"So, How Would You Rate This Year's Parade, Janelle?"

"It was okay, I guess," she said with a yawn.

Tom didn't give up. "It was better than that!" he said indignantly. "The only real lag I could see was between the dancing corn husks and the group from the juggling club."

Janelle was laughing now. "Those jugglers *always* hold things up. Did it all seem hopelessly hokey to you?"

He took her hand and held it tight. "It was fun. Sure, it was corny, but I liked it a lot." Now that she was smiling again, another thought entered his mind. "How long before the kids get back, Janelle?" He tried to sound casual but could tell from her expression that she was all but reading his thoughts.

"In about two hours." They stood up at the same time. Janelle watched him with a perfectly straight face. "I've got a whole album of pictures from the last few parades upstairs. Would you like to see them?"

Tom followed her into the house. "Do you think we have enough time?"

Janelle paused at the bottom of the steps. "Depends on how long we spend looking at pictures." She laughed before racing upstairs.

Dear Reader:

Welcome! You hold in your hand a Silhouette Desire—your ticket to a whole new world of reading pleasure.

A Silhouette Desire is a sensuous, contemporary romance about passions, problems and the ultimate power of love. It is about today's woman— intelligent, successful, giving—but it is also the story of a romance between two people who are strong enough to follow their own individual paths, yet strong enough to compromise, as well.

These books are written by, for and about every woman that you are—wife, mother, sister, lover, daughter, career woman. A Silhouette Desire heroine must face the same challenges, achieve the same successes, in her story as you do in your own life.

The Silhouette reader is not afraid to enjoy herself. She knows when to take things seriously and when to indulge in a fantasy world. With six books a month, Silhouette Desire strives to meet her many moods, but each book is always a compelling love story.

Make a commitment to romance—go wild with Silhouette Desire!

Best,

Isabel Swift
Senior Editor & Editorial Coordinator

MARY BLAYNEY
True Colors

Silhouette Desire

Published by Silhouette Books New York

America's Publisher of Contemporary Romance

SILHOUETTE BOOKS
300 East 42nd St., New York, N.Y. 10017

Copyright © 1988 by Mary Blayney

ISBN: 0-373-05448-3

First Silhouette Books printing September 1988

MARY BLAYNEY

is originally a child of the East Coast, having lived in New York and Washington, D.C., until her marriage. Then her life changed dramatically. In the past sixteen years her home has ranged from Muskegon, Michigan, to Juneau, Alaska, with visits to New Zealand and Fiji as well. Mary laughingly says that her list of previous employers is almost as varied as her addresses have been.

Mary enjoyed living in the Midwest and has drawn from her experiences there in creating the life-style in *True Colors*. As a writer, she has found a career as mobile as her family and hopes to use her travels in her future romance novels.

For Paul, Mike and Steve,
the men in my life

One

Tom Wineski gunned the engine and passed the truck he'd been following for the past five minutes. The two-lane road might be a main thoroughfare in this part of the country, but to a city boy it was little more than a side street. He revved the engine and estimated he would be in Jackson in less than five minutes.

The road was empty except for the truck rapidly fading into the distance, but the occasional country lane that intersected the state road and the endless rows of corn looked like the perfect spot for a speed trap. A speeding ticket was the last thing he needed. He'd worked too long and hard to avoid bad press, and the tabloids could make a federal case out of the most minor incident. With a sigh, Tom slowed down to fifty-five.

The road was flat and straight and didn't demand his full attention. Letting his mind drift, it settled on the last confrontation with his manager.

"Don't give them any trouble, Tom. No one's expendable, not even a star."

"I'm not talking trouble, Harris. Just three or four days to take care of personal business. It'll take longer than that to end the strike. It's not as if I'm the one holding up production."

"Okay, Tom." Harris's voice was matter-of-fact. "I know you've got problems, but straighten 'em out and get back here fast."

Despite his manager's concern, they both knew his spot on the show was solid. *Chicago's King* was the first bona fide hit that Kellen Productions had had in three years. They needed him as much, maybe even more, than he needed them.

He deliberately eliminated the rest of Harris's lecture from his mind. Instead, he thought about his lawyer, Katherine Howard. This was all her fault anyway. Why the hell did Katherine have to choose this particular week to visit family? A man expected his lawyer to be there when she was needed. First, her secretary refused to give out her number; then the woman tried to foist Katherine's paralegal on him. He wanted Katherine. He was paying big bucks for her expertise in this child custody suit, and he wanted Katherine to handle this and no one else.

The whole custody thing could blow sky-high any time, and she was off to enjoy rural America. Tom conceded she needed a break after the last case she'd handled. That case had attracted even more publicity than his would. Sure, she wasn't used to the kind of hounding she'd been getting from the press, but she'd better get used to it and fast. Now that she was a big-name lawyer, she would soon find the press was always around sniffing out the garbage.

He looked at the envelope lying on the seat beside him, glad that for once his over-organized attorney had forgotten a detail. He hadn't even needed the papers Katherine had forwarded to him, but the return address was his only hint of where he might find her. A phone call would have been a lot easier than this two-hour drive, but there'd been no name on the return address, just a street address and town. Nevertheless, it gave him a chance to test the rebuilt carburetor at something more than city speeds, he rationalized.

As he passed the sign announcing the town limits of Jackson, Wisconsin, Tom reduced his speed still further. Relaxing into his seat, he tried to ease the tension in his shoulders and neck. He was almost there. Though "there" wasn't much to speak of. The sign boasted that Jackson was the county seat with a population of five thousand.

He'd passed through a fair number of small towns in his time. Passed through being the operative phrase. Most weren't worth a second look, and this one was like all the rest. The main street was too modern to be quaint and too run-down to be attractive. But to his surprise it appeared to be thriving, if the number of people moving in and out of shops was any indication. It was like a caricature of every struggling small town he'd ever seen on the tube.

Tom slowed, debating whether to stop and ask directions. He decided against it. It might take a minute or two longer without them, but if he stopped to talk to the locals, he would surely be recognized. He made a left turn at the town's only traffic light and decided to cruise around a bit. Maybe he would come across the street sign he was looking for.

Off the main street and out of the business district the road was tree-lined and shady. The relative cool felt good. Distracted by the canopy of leaves and the slight breeze, he drove eight blocks, right out of town, without spotting a street sign for Whitewater. He opted for one more run through before asking for help. Pulling the steering wheel of the Porsche in a quick U, he groaned at the group of teens who cheered and applauded the maneuver. *Remember the low profile, Wineski.*

Checking the street signs more carefully this time, he found Whitewater, just two blocks off Main Street. Swinging a quick right, he found number 278 just two blocks down. He pulled in front of a white clapboard house and then rolled the car around the corner to take advantage of the late-afternoon shade.

The house sat toward the front of a large corner lot, and from his vantage point he could see the entire backyard. The grass looked healthy but dry. There was an empty clothesline and beyond that a mature vegetable garden. Rosebushes formed a hedge between the sidewalk and the backyard, and the smell of summer flowers drifted with the slight breeze. If he'd been a director looking for a location shot that captured small-town life, this backyard would be it.

Shaking off the thought, he considered whether to go to the front or back door. Catching movement on the back porch, he made his decision. Someone was working the rocking chair, probably Katherine's mother. He could see she was wearing an apron and fiddling with a bowl propped in her lap. The idyllic setting reminded him of a Norman Rockwell painting.

He sat in the car, forgetting his troubles, absorbing the feel of the place. For a moment he understood exactly why those five thousand people had chosen Jackson as home. His mind struggled for adjectives long unused: tranquil, stoic, basic, pleasant. His cynicism broke through his reverie—there was no place for him here. Besides, he rationalized, it was probably boring as hell.

He hoped he would find Katherine quickly, throw the news at her and be on his way to Chicago before dark. He pulled his long, lean frame out of the car, tried out a few smiles and headed toward the walk.

Janelle Harper watched the tall, thin man unfold himself from the battered sports car and groaned. Her expression didn't change. She went right on snapping the beans she'd just picked from the garden. But her mind went into overdrive as she tried to figure out how to deal with this latest intruder. Another nosy newspaperman. She could tell the type—full of big-city ego and insensitive to boot. He was the third one this week. Thank God Katherine and Rod had gone up to Door County. It was the only way they could have any time alone together with all the to-do over Katherine's latest case.

She watched him as he practiced smiling and decided his smile was just as insincere as the others' had been. She'd tried being nice; that hadn't worked on the Monday reporter. She'd tried being nasty, and the Wednesday creep had just out-nastied her. This time she would just act dumb.

Having decided on a course of action, she took a moment to assess the latest scavenger. Despite his thinness he was well built. His shoulders were muscular, as though he worked out with weights or swam or chopped wood. She gave his body a second look. Actually she was impressed. He really was in great shape. No bulge at the waistline like the guy on Wednesday, and his hair looked like his own. It was nice hair, too, a sable brown streaked with gold and a touch of silver.

His features weren't perfect, his nose was a little too big, his chin too square and his eyes were dominated by thick bushy brows. He conveyed a certain rugged, handsome virility that one didn't see very often, especially in Jackson. But there was more to it than that. She narrowed her eyes for a moment. He moved with a casual confidence that was close to arrogance. It was an aura Janelle associated with cowboys or venture capitalists, not that she'd ever met either.

As he approached the bottom of the porch steps, Janelle shifted in her seat, refusing to acknowledge the surge of attraction lurking on the edge of her annoyance. Instead she considered how best to start the conversation. Exactly what could she say that would sound noncommittal? She decided to let him speak first and take her lead from there.

Definitely not Katherine's mother, Tom decided. Dressed for the part, but too young. He glanced at her feet as he passed the edge of the porch, expecting to see sensible lace-up shoes. The bare feet with brightly polished toenails surprised him. How could a woman be vain enough to paint her

toenails yet wear a nondescript dress and pull her hair off
her face with no thought to style.

As he stopped at the bottom of the porch steps, he took
his first close look at her face and revised his opinion once
again. She couldn't be more than twenty-three. Could this
be Katherine's sister? She'd mentioned one just before she
left, a sister named Nell who lived in Wisconsin. *Sure*, that's
who this was. She had the same blond-brown hair, the same
hazel eyes, the same heart-shaped face. But this woman had
a light dusting of freckles across her nose and a gorgeous
mouth, something he'd never noticed when he looked at
Katherine. He wondered what she looked like beneath the
housedress she wore, then cut off his speculation, despite her
tempting mouth. A woman in his life was a complication he
didn't need.

He met her steady gaze and decided she was trying to figure out who he was. She would recognize him as soon as she
heard his voice. He turned on the full force of his charm,
determined to make points and win a smile.

"Good afternoon, ma'am." He slipped easily into the
voice and mannerisms of the man who'd made him famous
and waited a moment for recognition.

He scripted the scene in his mind. The bowl would fall to
the floor as she jumped up and fluttered and flustered
around the porch. He would spend a minute or two calming her down and then ask for Katherine.

Usually when he played a role he became absorbed in it,
but right now he seemed to stand apart from the character.
He was observing himself from some omniscient level,
judging his performance and gauging the reactions of the
woman in front of him.

"Hi," she responded, her guarded face cracking with the
beginnings of a smile. She sat fiddling with the beans in the
bowl, still rocking slowly back and forth. Her smile died
before it was fully born, and her eyes narrowed a little.

Tom felt the chill and revised his scenario. "I beg your
pardon, sorry to intrude on your afternoon, but I'm looking for Katherine Howard."

She kept right on rocking, considered his question and answered slowly. "I'm afraid I don't know anyone in town by that name. There are some Howards in Johnson's Creek, but their first names are Della and Bart."

Her line reminded him of a scene from a show about two months ago, and he wondered if she was remembering it, too. "King" had been looking for a drug dealer in a scruffy housing development. In the scene he'd confronted the dealer's woman and had gotten the information he wanted with a combination of macho charm and force.

Hell, if she wanted to play the scene, he would be happy to oblige. It wouldn't be the first time he'd entertained a fan that way.

He walked slowly up the short flight of steps, never taking his eyes off her face. At the intensity of his stare, she stopped rocking abruptly.

Pleased with the results of his scrutiny, Tom dredged up the next few lines of dialogue from his memory. As they surfaced, he sat casually on the porch railing. He didn't settle too comfortably; the damned thing wasn't as sturdy as it looked. There was more cynicism than menace in his voice, but the message was unmistakable. "You know who Katherine Howard is as well as I do. Much as I'd enjoy wrestling the information out of you, I'd appreciate it if you'd save us both time and energy and tell me where she is."

She practically threw the bowl of beans onto the table and stood up. "You arrogant idiot! There's no Kathleen Howard here, and there's not likely to be."

Tom straightened from the railing and took a step closer. "That's Katherine, honey. You remember her, your sister? I have a little slip of paper in the car that has this address. And you're her sister, Nell."

"Not Nell. It's Janelle." The woman winced at having even admitted that little bit of information and took a step backward, stepping behind the rocking chair as if it would provide protection.

He could feel the tension in the air. So she feels a little crowded, he thought. That's fine, just fine. Taking a step closer, he leaned across the table that separated them. He thought menacing, and a corresponding sneer stretched his lips with no illusion of humor. "Well then, Janelle, why don't you just go tell Katherine I'm here. I promise not to take up too much of her time. Just a couple of minutes, really."

His tone implied that the couple of minutes would be very unpleasant. That was stretching it a little, but truth to tell, the longer he stood there playing games with little Nell, the more annoyed he got with Katherine.

"I'm telling you, there's no Katherine here. I've said it three times, and I don't intend to say it again. Now why don't you just get in that little rust bucket of yours and pedal home?"

With that, Janelle stepped back from the table and turned abruptly. She pulled open the screen door and stepped inside. The door banged shut. She made no move to close the heavy inner door, nor did she lock the screen door. Tom took that as an invitation and followed her into the kitchen.

At the sound of the door banging again, Janelle whirled around to face him. Her eyes were narrowed once again, her lips compressed into thin lines and her hands clenched into fists at her sides. Tom wondered if maybe he'd misread the open door as an invitation. Then he reminded himself that she was living out a fantasy—acting—and doing a good job at it.

He didn't have to listen to her angry words. He knew she was telling him to get out of her house. He thought the words "conceited cretin" were a slight overstatement, but, after all, she was a beginner.

As he expected, she leaned over the table beside her and grabbed a steak knife, brandishing it at him. He thought it looked a lot more lethal than the flowerpot the TV character had wielded. He reviewed the choreography of the scene and decided that it wouldn't be hard to disarm her.

Before she had much of a chance to react, Tom grabbed her wrist and twisted it. He could feel the rapid pulse and wondered if she was as aware of him as he was of her. He applied a gentle pressure, forcing her to release the knife. It clattered to the floor, and Janelle turned her frightened eyes to him. She tried to step away from him, but he matched each of her steps with one of his own until he had her pinned against the refrigerator.

Tom took another step that brought his body into intimate contact with hers. He still held her right hand, and her other hand was effectively trapped between them. He could feel the heat of her body, her breasts pressed into his chest, her legs fit between his. He wanted to bury his hands in her hair, pull her closer so she could feel the urgency that had so distracted him.

"So much for the rough stuff, sweetheart. Why not just call Katherine and let's cut the rest of the scene?" Relaxing his punishing grip, he brought his arms up to rest on her shoulders, teasing the silken tendrils of hair that had escaped from her clip. "If we finish up the business, then maybe you and I can—"

His words were stopped by the look of panic in her eyes. He wanted to tell her to stop acting, that the scene was over. He watched her intently for a moment, taking in her panic-shaded fear.

Damn, he thought, she's not acting at all. And if she wasn't acting, then she really was as terrified as she looked. In that second he realized that what seemed so natural in front of the camera was pretty heavy stuff for a small-town girl. He'd threatened her, invaded her house and finally physically assaulted her. His embarrassment was an effective antidote to attraction. He released her and took a step back, groping for words to explain his actions.

Janelle didn't know why the man had changed his mind about attacking her, but her whole body sagged in relief. She felt her knees begin to buckle, and she slid down the refrigerator door, more than willing to wind up sitting on the floor.

Fear charged with adrenaline coursed through her as he once again reached for her. But instead of renewing his assault, he gently eased her into one of the chairs set near the table. She knew she should try to escape, at least try to reason with him, but she couldn't make herself move. She watched him as he took a glass from the place setting on the table and drew a glass of water.

He handed it to her with deliberate slowness and sat down across from her. "I think there's been a big mistake, Janelle, and it's all mine."

Janelle jerked her eyes from the serious contemplation of the glass in front of her and actually looked around the room, trying to identify the speaker. Is that why he'd backed off? Had someone else come in?

Her quick scrutiny showed no one else, and she looked at the man seated across from her. He was watching her as intently as before, but his arrogant contempt had been replaced by a gentle concern.

"Are you all right? Can I get you a cup of tea? Some brandy?"

She shook her head, refusing his offer. Janelle knew she looked totally confused. She was. Maybe this guy had some kind of weird split personality. He wasn't the same man she'd spent the past fifteen awful minutes with. She was afraid if she spoke he would change again.

"I'm Tom Wineski." His eyes searched her face as if looking for recognition, and he continued when she was silent. "I'm an actor. You must have heard of *Chicago's King*?"

Janelle nodded cautiously. Of course, she'd heard of the show. Every kid in Jackson was hooked on it. There was something about the Chicago cop and his rebellious behavior that appealed to youngsters. Tuesday nights had never been so quiet before. At least that's what her neighbor, a policeman, had said.

There was an edge of exasperation in Tom Wineski's voice as he continued. "Well, I'm 'King.' At least I play the role of the lead character. I thought you knew that and wanted to play out a scene opposite King. I don't normally use that, uh, approach." He paused a moment, running his hand across his face. "I can't believe I have to explain this all to you. There can't be a hundred people in America who wouldn't recognize King."

Janelle's feelings of panic had subsided, replaced by growing astonishment. "Let me get this straight. You assumed that I knew who you were? You thought I wanted a chance to play opposite this King character, and so you gave me a free audition?"

"Yeah." Tom nodded enthusiastically and smiled.

Janelle was certain it was his first sincere smile of the day. So, he was thrilled she was beginning to understand. She was beginning to understand a lot of things. Now all she wanted was to get rid of this man. His ego was taking up entirely too much space in her kitchen.

His smile was infectious though. It took a firm act of will not to return it. Instead she stood up, pleased that her legs did exactly what she told them. The enervating weakness of the last few minutes was gone. "I guess maybe I overreacted. There've been reporters around all week. I thought you were another one of those snoops."

"Me, a reporter? I could give you a few tips on keeping them at bay. I'll trade you for a lead on where I can find Katherine."

Janelle folded her arms across her chest and shook her head.

Apparently he read Janelle's resolution in her movements. He stood, too, and watched her, his smile fading. "It really is important for me to see her, and I gather she's not here."

"Absolutely not, Mr. Wineski. She deserves her vacation, and I can't imagine that anything you have to say can't wait two more days."

Before he could launch his next salvo, Janelle held up her hand. "I'm telling you there is absolutely no point in nagging. My twelve-year-old holds the world record for nagging, and it gets him nowhere. Come back tomorrow night, or better still, go back to Chicago and wait for Katherine to return your calls.''

''That's a low blow, Janelle, comparing me to a twelve-year-old. But I get the message. I have one myself, and she's made nagging a true art form.'' This time his accompanying smile was nostalgic, as though he missed even those unpleasant confrontations.

''I suppose it can wait a few days. Nothing much could happen over the weekend, anyway. I'm sorry about the mix-up. I didn't mean to scare you. Sometimes it's easier... Listen, no excuses. I'm sorry and I'll be in touch.'' With a nod of farewell he was out the door.

Janelle considered the unfinished sentence for a moment. The slam of the screen door as it swung back into place snapped her out of her reverie, and she stepped over to the door just in time to see him drive away.

She reviewed the scene on the porch and this time found some humor in it. She could imagine how those scenes usually ended. She'd never seen his show, but knew enough about the type to envision close shots of the hero and his current romantic interest.

Acknowledging to herself that this afternoon was as close as she would ever come to being King's ''current interest,'' she pushed the thought out of her mind and turned her full attention to stuffing the pork chops she'd planned to serve for supper.

As she closed the oven door, the back door banged open and her son, Dan, erupted into the room. ''Mom! Mom!'' His shouts echoed through the entire house.

For the hundredth time, Janelle wished her son would look around the kitchen before he shouted for her. To hear him yell, one might think she spent all her time in the crawl space that passed for an attic. With a long-suffering sigh she turned to her son. ''Dan, I'm right here.''

''Oh, yeah, I guess you are. I thought you might be in the bathroom or something and this is really important.''

"Dan, if this is about that old Mustang you want to buy and start fixing up, the answer is no. You won't be able to drive for years...."

"No, Mom." Dan waved his hand disparagingly, dismissing the subject that had occupied his attention for the past three weeks. "This is really *big* news, a late-breaking story, a really hot item. Guess who's in town? Right here in Jackson!"

"Tom Wineski." Her response was flat and humorless. Her lack of enthusiasm was lost on Dan as he looked at her in amazement.

"How did you know?"

"Just a lucky guess, Dan." *As a matter of fact, thirty minutes ago I was threatening him with a knife in this very kitchen.*

Janelle wondered if he heard her answer at all. His next questions drowned out her lame explanation. "Mom, what do you think he's doing here? Do you think he could be scouting out locations for next year's show? Wouldn't Jackson be a great spot to film?"

She smiled at the wistfulness in his voice. Personally, she couldn't think of many things worse than a TV production crew descending on the summer somnolence of Jackson. Janelle tried to look at it through his eyes. "It sure would, Dan. Think of all the business Uncle Ned would get at the convenience store. He might want to hire you like he does during Fall Fest."

"Yeah, and I was thinking they might need to hire extras for the show. Do you think so, Mom? Should I get my hair cut just in case they do auditions?"

"I don't think they do auditions for extras, son. And as much as I'd like to see you get a haircut, I really don't think Tom Wineski was here to stay. More than likely, he's just passing through."

"I guess you're right. But I gotta find Dennis Wilston and tell him anyway." He headed for the phone, but when it started ringing he made a sharp U-turn and made a beeline for the door instead. "I think I'll just run over to his house."

Janelle smiled. This summer her almost-seventh grader had been plagued by phone calls from the local girls who were just realizing what one of them had described as his "hunk potential." He dreaded the calls and almost never answered the phone.

This time it was more likely to be someone calling to tell her about the Wineski spotting. News traveled fast in a small town. Janelle wondered how long it would be before they figured out exactly where he'd spent his few minutes in Jackson.

She grabbed the phone on the third ring. "Hello, Harpers'."

"Why the hell did they name a motel 'Rooster's Rest'?"

Janelle sank into the chair by the phone, her legs experiencing the same weak-kneed failure they had earlier. As one part of her brain answered, another part thought about Tom Wineski's hunk potential. "It's on the site of the county's first and only chicken ranch. The owners thought it would help folks remember its place in local history. Are you planning on staying then?"

"Yeah, I thought I'd at least wait until tomorrow and be one step ahead of all of Katherine's messages. The man at the desk gave me a room with a view." He paused a moment. "Janelle, the view is of the interstate."

The disbelief in his voice tempered her dislike. He was like an alien visitor. Given his life-style, it was easy to imagine that Jackson was another world for him.

"You sound just like I felt when I first came here. After a while it begins to make sense, though. To old Neil at the desk, those rolling hills meant nothing but work. The interstate not only changed his land, but it changed his life, gave him a way out."

The silence on the other end of the line made her rush on. "I'm sorry, I didn't mean to lecture. I just wanted—"

"No, no, I was thinking about what you said. I guess that means you haven't lived here all your life. Is your husband from Jackson?"

"Actually, he was. But I didn't move here until after he died. But after living here five years, I feel like a native."

She couldn't believe that she was beginning to feel sorry for a man who, less than an hour ago, had scared her to death. She halfheartedly considered inviting him to dinner, but crushed that idea fast.

She hurried to end the conversation. "Thanks for calling. I promise to give Katherine the message as soon as she and Rod get back, but I really don't expect them before late tomorrow night, maybe even Sunday night."

There was a moment of silence on the other end, and Janelle wondered if maybe he'd called with hopes of a dinner invitation.

"Listen, I want to beat the dinner rush at the local tavern. According to Neil, Friday night means fish fry. I wouldn't want to miss my weekly overdose of cholesterol. I guess I better go. See you tomorrow night."

A stirring of guilt edged its way into her consciousness as she broke the connection. It really was heartless to condemn any man to the crowds at the Friday night fish fry.

Let him suffer.

But she shifted uncomfortably at the thought. She should have at least warned him that he'd been spotted and the locals were on the lookout. His car might have been a rusting heap of gray metal, but it was hard to miss a Porsche in Jackson, even one that had seen better days.

He was bound to be used to it. He probably loved the attention. If he really wanted to go unnoticed, he would drive an old station wagon or a pickup.

The phone rang again, shaking her out of her reverie. This time it was one of Dan's admirers. After taking a message from the caller, this one interspersed with breathless giggles, she headed for the front door, hoping to find the afternoon paper. As she reached the door, she heard the familiar thump of the paper hitting the mat. She opened the door in time to call a thank-you to the carrier. He waved back.

The simple gesture reminded her of how much she liked living in Jackson. People took the time to really see one another. If that friendliness sometimes crossed the border into nosiness, it was a small price to pay for the knowledge that you were never alone. So what if everyone found out that Tom Wineski had stopped by her house? She didn't have anything to hide.

She settled on the living room couch and turned to the funnies. Nothing like the comics in the *Milwaukee Journal* to take your mind off life's real problems.

No point in overstating the situation, Janelle chastised herself. A "real problem" wasn't the right way to describe Tom Wineski. With the paper resting in her lap, Janelle considered a few alternative phrases: perhaps something like a "minor irritation." She recalled the waves of attraction she'd felt and decided that didn't do him justice. Maybe an "annoying interruption." No, not that bad, not when she could laugh at the episode. How about "an absurd fantasy," maybe even "an amusing interlude?" On second thought, Janelle decided, maybe "real problem" was the best description, after all.

Two

Tom hoisted himself onto the windowsill. Using the edge of the tub for balance, he pushed his six-foot-two-inch frame through the small bathroom window. A moment later he jumped carefully onto the narrow ledge of dirt that surrounded the motel. The last thing he needed was to twist his ankle. A three-mile run would be easy enough as long as he didn't lose his footing on the unfamiliar terrain and twist his knee or sprain his ankle.

Sliding down the steep hill that gave the motel its wonderful view of the interstate, he crouched at the bottom, listening for any signs that he'd been discovered. Satisfied that he'd made his escape undetected, he headed for the church spire in the distance and Janelle Harper's house.

He avoided the main road and ran close to the corn rows on a less prominent roadway. It was true that it would be easier to trip, but he could also jump into the field corn if a car came along.

He swore to himself as he settled into a familiar even pace. He wasn't sure if he was angry at himself for not realizing what the tavern would be like or at Janelle for not warning him in advance.

The place had been smoke-filled and relatively dark, and Tom had hoped he could pass unrecognized. He hadn't counted on the two kids at the bar who spotted him almost instantly. Wasn't it illegal for kids to be in a bar if they weren't old enough to drink? Whatever, these two kids were sitting at the bar playing checkers as he walked in. The game was quickly forgotten when they recognized him.

Tom Wineski! The words rippled through the crowd and he smiled weakly. When he realized they were interested in Tom Wineski, USC tight end and former Los Angeles Ram he relaxed considerably. It'd been years since anyone had mentioned his football days and it was a pleasant change.

What memories these people had! They remembered plays he'd forgotten years ago. They remembered stats sports announcers had to be reminded of. He wondered why they were sitting in a bar when they could make their fortunes in sports trivia.

It'd been fun for the first ten minutes, trading stories and remembering the good times. Then someone began to press him about his injuries and early retirement. One of them had even brought up the custody suit. It was then he'd decided he'd better forget dinner and leave. He'd done it as gracefully as he could, signing a few more autographs, working his way toward the door and back to his car, hoping the local fast-food place had a drive-up window.

He stopped back at the motel to call his daughter, but the line was busy. By the time he was ready to leave again, there was a group of ten teenage girls gathered outside his door. He stayed hidden behind the curtains until he was able to get through to his daughter, or rather the answering machine. By then the crowd had doubled, and they were chanting something unintelligible. That was when he decided that the bathroom window would make a safer exit than the door.

At least it was a nice afternoon for a run. The weather was cooling quickly, although the sun was still in the sky. He let his mind wander as he found a comfortable footing on the hard-packed dirt. He liked running. Thoughts came randomly. Sometimes he observed the world around him, sometimes he solved a few problems, but always the exertion felt good.

A mammoth building on his left was cast into shadow by the setting sun. Some kind of factory, he guessed. It must have had something to do with corn, since huge silo-like buildings made up the bulk of the structure. As he passed the main gate, he looked for a sign. Who needed a sign, he reasoned, when he didn't see one. Everyone in town knew what it was. He would ask Janelle.

Janelle. So she'd buried herself up here when her husband died. He wondered if it was out of grief or to punish herself. He wondered if she was in the "lonely widow" class and would be interested in a little personal attention. *Shelve that idea, buddy, let's not confuse this situation any more than it already is.* He concentrated on his breathing for a moment, annoyed with his thoughts. Besides, she wasn't the type for a fling, anyway.

When you looked beyond the rural costume and casual hairstyle, she was dynamite. She must be older than twenty-three if she had a twelve-year-old son, but she sure didn't look it. There were those sparkling eyes and that scattering of freckles. And that sweetly sensual mouth.

Maybe if she fixed herself up, she would have some of Katherine's dramatic good looks. On the other hand, women with that sophisticated veneer were a dime a dozen. He liked Janelle Harper just the way she was, right down to those silly painted toenails. Just the memory of her body pressed into his was enough to send a shudder through him. Undressing her would be like taking the plain brown wrapping off an issue of *Playboy*. He shook his arms, then broke into a sprint trying to eliminate the excess energy.

Here he was, imagining her naked beside him, and he would be lucky if she even spoke to him. What a beginning. It had been an absurd confrontation. The Norman Rockwell fantasy had faded fast. It had been more like Norman Bates for a few minutes there. And all because she hadn't known who he was. He tried to recall a time when his name hadn't been all he'd needed to get almost anything he'd wanted. Since his sophomore year in high school, he guessed, when he'd been the sole reason his high school had won the state football championship. Now he'd met someone who not only didn't recognize him or his name, but thought he was a jerk on top of it. He smiled and shook his head. Why did that make him feel so good?

After another half mile, he reached the suburban outskirts of Jackson. He checked for the spire and headed toward the church, watching for street signs and possible recognition at the same time.

By sticking to the back streets, he was able to avoid detection. He gave the ice-cream stand a wide berth and went at least four blocks out of his way to avoid the town's main intersection, arriving at the Harpers' back door barely out of breath. He could hear someone talking, and he stepped closer to the door, unabashedly eavesdropping.

Cradling the phone between her head and shoulder, Janelle grabbed the oven mitt lying on the counter. If the pork chops stayed in a minute longer, they would be overdone. She jerked the oven door open and pulled out the pan while carrying on her part of the conversation. Since all that was required of her was an occasional "yes" or "no" or "hmm," she was able to do both things at once.

Janelle loved her mother-in-law. She was everything to her that her own mother had never been. Irene Harper had been "Mom" to her since the first year she and Arnie had married. Irene Harper loved the telephone almost as much as she loved her children. Janelle figured it came from all those years growing up on the farm without one. Irene was still thrilled that she could talk to any of her four children and eight grandchildren without leaving her kitchen. She called everyday, even on the days when she saw them, sometimes just to make sure their phones were working.

But Mom had a real reason to call today. Right now she was reviewing every bit of evidence possible to support her belief that Tom Wineski was really staying in Jackson. Janelle settled into a chair trying to calculate how long the chops would stay warm.

"I ask you, Janelle, would the man stop in at the tavern, for dinner, mind you, if he was just passing through?"

"You saw him at the tavern?"

"Not me, but Ned did, and Kathy called and told me."

It figures, Janelle thought. As the eldest daughter, Kathy reported all the big news to Irene.

"Yes, and Ned talked to him one-on-one about his football career—"

"Now wait, Mom, the guy's an actor, not a football player."

"Oh, Nell, there are times when I can tell you're not really from Wisconsin. If you'd grown up here you couldn't help but know that Tom Wineski was a football player. That was before his acting got started."

Janelle tried to figure out why she found that useless piece of information fascinating, then resolved to forget it as soon as possible. She glanced at the rapidly cooling pork chops. "Mom, I'm sorry, but I have to go. Dinner's all ready and I heard Dan on the back porch a minute ago. I'm glad Ned got a chance to talk to this guy. I wish I had something to add to the tale, but he hasn't been spotted east of the ice-cream stand." Janelle felt a twinge of guilt at the fib, but knew it was in everyone's best interest to keep Tom's reason for being in town in low profile.

She hung up the phone and turned to greet her son as the back door creaked open. Instead, Tom Wineski slipped through the door and smiled. "You better watch out. Remember what happened to Pinocchio when he told lies."

His smile was irresistible. She wanted to be annoyed, but it was hard to sound angry when your mouth refused to be stern. "Now, what do you want?"

As if on cue, his stomach growled. Not a delicate little grumble, but a long drawn-out rumble. Janelle watched as his face turned red, and she burst out laughing as he added, "Those pork chops sure smell good."

She controlled her laughter with some effort. The fact that he stood there eyeing her with an almost hurt expression helped. Finally, she bit her lip and reduced the chuckles to a smile.

"I guess they never got around to serving you at the tavern." At that she started laughing again. She could just imagine the way he eyed the platters of fish that passed him by while the locals discussed his career.

This time it was easier to control the laughter. He was beginning to look annoyed. "I guess you can eat with us. I made extra. But first you better put your car in the garage or you won't be safe even here. This is a small town and—"

"Janelle, one thing I've figured out by now is that this is a small town. I didn't drive, I just jogged over from the motel." As he spoke, he moved farther into the room and took the silverware Janelle had taken from the drawer and began to set his own place between the two already there. Janelle wondered if he felt the electricity as their hands touched. She tried to keep up her end of the conversation, but the tingle had generated a chain reaction that left her breathless.

"You ran from down by the interstate? You must be exhausted."

"No, not really. I can run about five miles a day easily. I figured it was about three miles here. I'll probably be able to run back later."

She handed him a napkin and a water glass just to test her reaction again. It's still there, she thought. "We'll see about that later. If you want to wash up, you can use the bathroom upstairs. The towels are in the cabinet to the left of the sink."

He nodded and headed toward the front of the house. Janelle sighed as she watched him leave. She arched her eyebrows and rubbed her forehead, a sure sign that she was facing a problem she wasn't sure how to handle. The last time she felt that way was when Dan had brought a snake home as a pet. Handling that had been a piece of cake compared to this. Tom Wineski was no snake, but he definitely didn't fall into the pet class, either. She hoped he would eat and leave. She knew he wouldn't.

She realized she was making mountains out of mole-hills—the guy was just hungry. But his eyes were sending entirely different messages, messages she was having no trouble interpreting.

It's habit, Janelle. You can't imagine he'd be attracted to you when he has his pick of Chicago beauties.

She felt a little embarrassed at her wishful thinking.

She turned off the argument, determined to give the man what he wanted—dinner. Rummaging through the refrigerator, she found a leftover beer from the Fourth of July barbecue. She put that with a pilsner glass at Tom's place and sat down to wait for his return, trying to think up suitable dinnertime conversation. Avoid politics and religion, she reminded herself, and remembering his association with her sister, the state of the American family might not be too good a choice, either.

Of course, if Dan were here, she wouldn't have to worry about a thing. She knew better than to hope her son would be on time. He was always late. Maybe he'd eat at Dennis Wilston's, and Tom would be gone before he got home.

The back door creaked open and slammed shut. "Mom! Mom!" Dan yelled before catching sight of her seated at the kitchen table. "This is awesome! Tom Wineski is staying at the Rooster's Rest! Mom, he's staying in town for at least one night. Can I ride my bike over there and get his autograph?"

Janelle was tempted to send him off. The fewer people who knew why Tom Wineski was in town, the quieter her life would be. On the other hand, if Tom was going to be around all weekend, she knew Dan would find out sooner or later.

"No, Son, you may *not* ride your bike over there." As he was about to protest, she held up her hand. "No, you may not walk, ride your skateboard or hitchhike. You can wash your hands and sit down and eat dinner."

She watched him walk over to the sink. She could tell by the rigid way he held his head and neck that he was angry with her. He didn't say a word but turned on the faucet full force and washed his hands with elaborate care.

It reminded Janelle of Dan's father. Arnie had withdrawn into himself just the same way when she'd annoyed him. Dan couldn't even remember that. It was funny the way some behavior patterns repeated themselves. Dan turned back to the table. Apparently he didn't like her smile. His eyes narrowed and his sullen expression deepened. He eyed the third place setting with annoyance.

"Who else is eating over?" Resentment boiled over into his tone of voice. "I don't feel like being polite. It better not be anyone I have to be nice to."

Janelle's smile grew broader as she heard Tom coming downstairs. He whistled tunelessly and entered the kitchen just as Dan took a long gulp of milk.

The twelve-year-old's eyes grew large, and he all but choked on the milk as he jumped up from the table, his chair falling to the floor. Janelle decided that the enthusiasm of Dan's recognition more than made up for her initial coolness. She shook her head and smiled as the man and boy exchanged handshakes and seated themselves at the table.

Conversation was no problem. Dan was full of a thousand questions about *Chicago's King*, and Tom answered them with good grace. Janelle sat back and listened to the conversation, watching the two interact.

"*King* is my all-time favorite TV show. It's really fun when we go down to Chicago and see all the places you use in the show, you know, like the Field Museum and all those train tracks."

Tom nodded, and Dan kept right on talking, usually with his mouth full.

"Sometimes it seems strange that King became a cop at all. I mean he's always fighting with his bosses, and most of his friends are real lowlifes, you know?" He looked at Tom expectantly, apparently waiting for an explanation.

"I guess you never saw the pilot show."

Dan gave his mother a disgusted look. "No, Mom wouldn't let me stay up that late when I was seven. I only started watching about three years ago."

"You didn't miss much. The pilot was the only good thing about those first couple of years. The guy who wrote the pilot didn't write any scripts until two seasons later. Until then I wasn't sure the show was going to make it. I think it hung on initially because there wasn't much competition on Tuesday night."

"Yeah, it was kind of weird the way it suddenly got real popular after it'd been on a while."

Dan had given up all pretense at eating. He continued conducting his interview with all the skill of a network reporter with a time limit.

"So, anyway, how come King's a cop?"

Tom appeared to be answering his questions with patience, explaining King's misspent youth—always on the fringe of the law. He'd become a cop when his younger brother had been killed, using it as a means to get revenge, but soon finding the department was the only place he could legally use the dubious skills he'd learned in a lifetime spent on the streets.

As Janelle watched, she realized that once again he'd slipped into his show-business persona, the artificial smile, the voice that belonged to a character and not Tom Wineski. His body language was King's, too. She wondered if he even realized it.

It occurred to her that the treatment he was receiving from Dan was not all that different from the way the folks at the tavern had reacted. Just as Dan was starting to ask him why he was in Jackson, Janelle intervened. "Son, why don't you eat your dinner and let Tom eat his. You know he drove all the way up from Chicago, and he told me a little while ago he was starved. Maybe you can finish this conversation later."

They ate in silence for a few moments. The silence grew strained, and Janelle struggled to think of a topic of mutual interest that didn't center on acting. "Tom, was that a Porsche you were driving before?"

That was all she needed to say. Within five minutes Dan and Tom were engrossed in a discussion of cars and car parts that definitely did not include her. She didn't mind. Tom was relaxed, and Dan's animation came from his interest in cars and not from awe at being in the presence of a well-known celebrity.

As Dan stood to clear the table and get the pie for dessert, Tom turned to Janelle. "You really should buy that car he wants. A 1969 Mustang convertible really is a collector's item."

What a traitor. I get him off an uncomfortable subject and this is how he rewards me. Tom didn't notice her lack of enthusiasm.

"Janelle, if you want, I could go take a look at it for you. Dan says the body is still in good shape, and the engine work would be good experience for him."

Dan stood at his place, looking at her with an innocent expression. Once again it reminded her of how Arnie looked when he knew he had her in a tight spot. She addressed her son before turning to Tom.

"You know, Dan, a little earlier today, Tom and I had a discussion about nagging. Now I can see I'm going to have to have a little talk with him about the way adults are supposed to support each other, and not side with the kids."

"But, Janelle—"

"'But' doesn't work with my Mom, Tom. Maybe we better drop the subject for a while." The boy accompanied his words with a vigorous nod that encouraged agreement, then plunked the pie onto the table.

They finished the meal with a good-natured argument about the merits of apple pie versus the peach pie that Irene had brought over earlier that day. Dan insisted that Tom wait to try his grandma's apple pie before deciding that the peach was tops on the list.

Tom insisted on helping Dan clear the table and then asked if he could help Janelle with the dishes while Dan disappeared upstairs to look for the back issue of a car magazine he and Tom had discussed.

As Tom stood by the sink waiting for the first round of wet plates, Janelle admitted to herself that she enjoyed the companionable silence and tried to ignore the feelings his closeness aroused.

She handled the dinner plates with extra care. Her hands seemed less steady than usual. Instead of handing him the wet plate, she put it in the dish drainer. There was too much electricity in the space between them to risk direct contact. If she touched him again, she was afraid her whole body would short-circuit.

Come on, Janelle, she argued with herself, he's just a man. Treat him like Ned. Good old balding, heavyset Ned, probably the best brother-in-law in the world.

You're right. This is ridiculous. But just look at him standing there. He has no right to look that good.

This is ridiculous, Tom thought to himself. He was feeling like an oversexed school boy, while Janelle was standing there calmly doing the dishes. After one home-cooked meal all he could think about was how great her figure was and how beautiful her neck looked with her hair up like that. Tom had never thought of pork chops as an aphrodisiac. At that thought, he laughed out loud, and Janelle turned startled eyes toward him.

He cleared his throat, using the moment to search his mind for an appropriate cover. "I'll never forget Dan's expression when I walked into the kitchen. It was priceless."

"It was definitely the highlight of his day, probably of the summer."

Janelle turned back to the sink again, and Tom watched her hands as she carefully washed each dish. He envisioned her using the same gentle technique on his body, and then forced his mind elsewhere.

He glanced around the kitchen, pausing to examine it carefully. "You know, this is really an interesting kitchen. It looks like it hasn't been touched in fifty years. I mean this black linoleum dates back to the forties at least. And the enamel cabinets are from the same time period, I'd guess. There isn't even a dishwasher.''

Janelle handed him another dish and smiled. "Oh, I have a portable, but I only use it on big occasions when I have lots of company and lots of dishes.''

She turned back to the sink and talked while she finished the plates. Tom half listened while attempting to count the number of pins that kept her hair up. "I don't mind washing dishes by hand most of the time.''

Tom interrupted his pin count. "The thing is, the style is old, but everything looks brand-new. How do you keep it from aging?''

She looked over her shoulder once again, and Tom forgot all about the hairpins and smiled back as she continued. "I like the kitchen like this, the simplicity of it, so whenever something wears out, I just replace it in kind.

"I got the idea about three years ago when I found an old refrigerator in a barn at an estate sale. It was forty years old and had never been uncrated, and they were selling it for almost nothing. It was about the time my old refrigerator was developing a death rattle. I replaced it with the one I found. At another farm sale I found a box of black linoleum. I didn't need it then, but I bought it and kept it until last year when the floor needed to be replaced.''

"You just like going to auctions and that kind of thing?'' He was leaning against the counter now, right next to the sink where Janelle was endlessly scouring a broiling pan. With her attention fixed on the dirty dish, he watched her as she spoke, enjoying the sound of her voice, the curve of her neck. When she glanced up to answer his question, he noticed that her eyes weren't hazel at all, but blue.

"Actually, going to auctions and estate sales is my job.''

"You mean you buy antiques?''

She nodded, all her attention seemingly focused on a spot of grease that looked at least three years old.

"How'd you get into that?''

"When I first came here, I did volunteer work at a charity thrift store. One day a lady brought in some old linens that I was sure would be worth a lot more in the city. I told her so, but she still wanted to donate them, so I called my sister Katherine and found an antique store in Chicago. The store made a better profit than they would have if I'd sold them locally.

"A few weeks later the shop owner came by and asked if I wanted to buy for them. I said sure. It's a great job. It takes me all over this part of the state, but I can structure the schedule anyway I want, so I can still be here for Dan, or help my mother-in-law with canning, or take time off when Katherine visits. Other than that, you can usually find me at sales or in the kitchen."

The phone rang, and Janelle moved quickly to answer it, wiping her hands on the towel Tom was holding.

Tom grabbed the last pan in the rack and calculated it had been a good ten years since he'd met a woman who admitted to spending most of her time in the kitchen. He tried to envision some of his dates even walking into the kitchen, much less knowing what to do once they got there.

He amended that. On second thought, they might know what to do but it wouldn't be the dishes. Kitchens were all right if variety was what you wanted, but personally he would prefer the brass bed he'd glimpsed on his quick trip upstairs. He'd glanced only briefly but had been intrigued by the huge bed and large oak armoire angled in the corner. An elegantly upholstered chaise longue near a fireplace added to the sensual feeling of the room. The Janelle he envisioned in her bedroom was entirely different from the woman who'd made pork chops and then washed the dishes without a thought to her manicure. The pale peach teddy hanging on a hook in the bathroom had only fired his imagination.

As his body began to respond to his imagination, he decided it would be better for him to listen to Janelle's conversation than continue his present train of thought.

"I'm sorry. I don't know who could have told you he was here." She paused a moment. "Please, it's not worth crying over." She paused again. "Wait just a minute, there's, uh, someone at the door."

She covered the receiver carefully and turned to Tom. Her expression reminded him of the bean-snapping, knife-wielding woman he'd first encountered. "I don't think that I can take a whole weekend of this. This is a girl named Tippy. She insists she's your daughter and that you gave her this number."

Tom's casual stance disappeared, and he leaped for the phone, grabbing the receiver from her hand and pulling the rest of the phone off the counter. "Tippy, honey, it's Daddy. What's the matter?"

For a moment all he heard were sniffles and the hiccuping sound she made when she cried. It was obvious she was upset, and his concern grew. She cried all the time these days. It was one of the things that worried him most. He waited a moment longer and tried to get her to talk again.

"Daddy, Mrs. Meltzer has to go to Milwaukee to be with her daughter who's having a baby. We don't know what to do. I tried calling you at the first number for hours, but no one answered. So then I tried the second number. And that lady said you weren't there at first...."

Tom considered letting her finish her story. Then he decided it might take another twenty minutes. This kind of blow-by-blow account was a trait she'd inherited from her mother. No wonder he disliked it so much. "Listen, honey, you can tell me the rest later. What's the problem? I didn't realize you were so attached to Mrs. Meltzer." He knew darn well Mrs. Meltzer wouldn't win any popularity contests. God help her, the old lady had to be as tough as old army boots or Elaine would have walked all over her months ago.

Tippy gave a watery giggle. "Daaaddy. It's not that. It's that Mom went to one of those parties last night. And I don't know when she'll be home. I don't want to stay here alone. Besides, Cliff is living here now, and I don't like him."

Boy, when she gets to the punch line, she really delivers. Tom tried to assimilate all the information she'd loaded into that last exchange. He relayed it back to her and tried to keep the growing anger from his voice. "Let me get this straight. Mrs. Meltzer is taking the bus to Milwaukee, and your mother is at one of those three-day parties, I assume with Cliff. Didn't she leave a number?" He scooped the phone off the counter and began pacing the room.

"Daddy, of course she did and I tried calling. They said she was too stoned or too drunk to come to the phone. The guy who answered offered to get Cliff, but I—"

Once again Tom cut her off. He hated it when she sounded so world-weary. "Okay, honey. Why don't you let me talk to Mrs. Meltzer?"

There was a bit of muffled conversation, then the lightly accented voice of the housekeeper.

"Mr. Wineski? This is Anna Meltzer. I tried to get Tippy to let me make the call, but she wouldn't let me have the phone number. I told her I really didn't care where you were and had no intention of passing any information about your personal life along to your ex-wife, but she insisted on making the call herself."

The woman continued talking without so much as a breath.

"I just don't know what to do. My daughter needs me and the taxi will be here any minute. I can't leave this child here alone."

"I appreciate that, Mrs. Meltzer, and I'll get there as soon as I can. Surely Tippy can take care of herself for a couple of hours."

He heard Mrs. Meltzer conveying the plan to Tippy, then the child was back on the line.

"Daddy, why can't I just come there? It will take you hours to get home, and by then it'll be the worst part of the night."

He hated the fear in her voice enough to consider the option. "I suppose you could come here, honey, but there isn't any time to arrange a ride."

"Oh God, Daddy, the taxi's here. What am I going to do?"

He tried not to react to the panic in her voice. "Calm down, Tippy. The taxi will just have to wait until I figure out what to do." He was about to ask her to put Mrs. Meltzer back on, when Janelle thrust a sheet of paper under his nose. *The Milwaukee bus stops in Jackson.*

His whole body sagged in relief. "Listen, Tippy. Let me talk to Mrs. Meltzer a moment and go tell the cabdriver to wait. This will only take a minute."

There was a burst of confusion on the other end and he was afraid they'd hung up. Then he heard Mrs. Meltzer's voice. He calmed himself and tried for a diplomatic tone of voice.

"I know you're in a hurry, Mrs. M., but could you please take Tippy with you on the bus and let her off in Jackson? That's where I'm staying. We'll be at the bus station to meet her."

Relief was evident in the woman's voice. "Of course, Mr. Wineski. I'd be happy to do it. But we'll have to hurry, or I won't have time to buy her a ticket."

"Hey, leave a note for Elaine...." His voice trailed off as he realized she'd broken the connection. Replacing the phone on the counter, he turned to face Janelle. He felt as though he'd run three miles backward. She must have read his mind. Handing him the last of his dinner beer, she smiled in sympathy as he drained it in one gulp.

"I'm awfully sorry about that, Tom. I had no idea it was your daughter. I'm afraid I *did* give her the runaround."

"No problem, Janelle. I should have gotten in touch with Tippy before I left Chicago, but I didn't envision being gone that long. Then the line was busy. When I did get through, I got the answering machine. You'd think with all the money I pay for child support, Elaine would get a second telephone number."

At the mention of his ex-wife's name, all the anger he'd been trying to suppress came surging back. He slammed his fist onto the counter. A string of epithets came to mind, but he resisted voicing them in deference to the woman standing nearby.

"Do you believe she's at a weekend party with her latest live-in boyfriend? What kind of example is that for Tippy? How can any judge consider Elaine a fit mother?" He looked over at Janelle who sat in one of the chairs by the table. Her forbearance annoyed him, and he raised his voice, hoping for a reaction that would let him vent his increasing anger. "Don't you have anything to say?"

"No. Actually, I thought I'd just listen awhile." Then she smiled. It was an expression he was beginning to recognize. When he was being arrogant, self-centered and bad-tempered, she would smile that tolerant smile and aim a few well-chosen words his way. His anger drained away.

God, he'd seen that smile at least twice already, and he'd only met her six hours ago. Talk about great first impressions. She was treating him like her twelve-year-old son.

Maternally.

His thought process took an abrupt turn as the adjective flashed through his mind. Was that how she felt about him? Motherly? Hell, she was the only damn woman in America who felt that way. Here he'd spent a good part of the past two hours admiring her appeal, admiring her body, even admiring her bed, and her thoughts were *maternal*?

He walked over to where she sat. He stood directly in front of her, his body blocking escape. He leaned against the refrigerator and smiled down at her. "End of temper tantrum." His grin broadened. "You know, I've been wondering how long your hair is and exactly how many pins you have stuck in there to keep it up." He reached behind her and pulled out the one or two pins that had worked their way loose.

Janelle's sweet smile disappeared, and a squint of uncertainty mixed with surprise lit her eyes. He was so close that their knees were touching. He'd never thought of knees as

particularly erotic, but even that nominal contact was affecting him. He could tell she was feeling it, too. Then the
room erupted in noise.

"Tom, Tom," Dan's bellow preceded him. As he burst
into the kitchen, the shouting stopped. "Oh, there you are.
I thought maybe you went outside. Sorry it took so long. I
had to go up to the attic. But I found two other issues that
talk about old Mustangs. Come on into the dining room. We
can spread out there."

He turned from the boy and gave Janelle a look of parental resignation. Her nervousness disappeared, and she
smiled back, though not a maternal smile this time. She
threw her hands over her heart in a classic Victorian gesture, and her smile grew wider as she said, "Saved by the
boy." Then she burst out laughing.

Three

Janelle watched the man and the boy as her son babbled on about engines and car design. Still sitting in the chair near the kitchen table, she had a direct view of the two of them bent over the dining room table. Tom was following Dan's conversation and gestures with halfhearted interest.

Janelle could tell he was worried about his daughter by the way Tom kept looking at his watch and how often Dan had to repeat his comments. Janelle watched a moment longer and decided that tonight was not the night to start plans for another major auto company.

"Dan," she called from her chair, "I think it's about time for the root-beer floats, don't you?"

She got up and walked to the dining room, praying that Dan would acquiesce gracefully. Swimming was important to Dan. She decided to use that approach. "How about saving that discussion for tomorrow. You know you have a swim meet in the morning. Coach Harrelson thinks you have a real chance of leading your age group, and it'd be a shame to blow it."

The boy was ready to argue, but help came from an unexpected quarter. "Your Mom's right, Dan. I remember when I played football. I felt like a baby, but I really needed ten hours of sleep the night before a game. Look, I'll help you clean this up and it'll take half the time." The two set about sorting the papers into neat piles, but not before Janelle caught the wink Tom aimed at her.

Janelle set out the fixings for root-beer floats and hoped that the quiet family routine would help Tom relax. She poured the soda into glasses, added the ice cream, then topped off the float with more root beer. The vanilla-flavored fizz dribbled down the side of the glass just as it always did, and Dan came in just in time to chastise his mother for her sloppiness. It was all part of the ritual.

In a few minutes the three were settled on the back porch. The two adults claimed the rocking chairs on either side of the wooden table, and the boy sat on the porch, leaning his body against the loose railing. They sat in silence, absorbing the night sounds. There were a few birdcalls in the gathering twilight, and the cicadas and crickets were beginning their endless nightsong. Occasionally a car would cruise down the street or a bike rider would whiz by. It was a perfect summer night in Jackson, Wisconsin.

Janelle turned to Tom, but didn't speak. He sat with his eyes closed, rocking slowly back and forth. He looked relaxed, his mouth expressionless, his only movement the flexing of his leg muscles.

If the scene had been a painting, Janelle would have titled it *Terminal Boredom*. He would relax all right; he would probably go right to sleep. Janelle imagined it was pretty different from the way Tom usually spent his Friday nights.

The fact that this evening tradition was the highlight of her week made her feel even more uncomfortable. Usually she and Dan would discuss plans for the weekend. Sometimes the conversation would last a few minutes, sometimes a few hours. But tonight their whole routine had been changed by Tom Wineski's arrival. First she'd been angry, then frightened, confused, amused and finally attracted.

Now she was embarrassed. Root-beer floats on the back porch. She was amazed he hadn't burst out laughing when she'd suggested it. She forgot all about her intention to make him relax and feel comfortable. Instead she just felt like a fool.

"Listen, Janelle, maybe you better tell me what your weekend plans are. Tippy and I don't want to interfere with anything you have going on."

He *had* to be kidding. He'd turned her world upside down from the first moment he'd stepped onto the porch. She looked at him, trying to gauge his sarcasm quotient.

"It's no problem," Dan volunteered. "I have a swim meet tomorrow morning, but I should be home by ten. Then maybe we could go check out the Mustang."

"Now, just a minute, Son." Janelle interrupted. "The lawn needs mowing, and you're being paid to weed the Turners' garden before we go to Grandma's on Sunday, and you promised Uncle Ned that you'd help clean the alley behind the store."

"Oh geez, Mom, I don't feel like cutting the grass." He gave up as she raised her hand in the familiar gesture. "Okay, okay, I guess I'll go to bed." He stood up, pushing extra hard on the rickety railing and knocking over his glass in the process. Without a word he went into the house, allowing the door to slam behind him.

The adults sat in silence for a moment, watching the glass roll to a standstill. Janelle, embarrassed by Dan's display of bad temper, avoided eye contact with Tom.

"If it's any consolation, Tippy and I have the same conversations. They sure don't make it easy, do they?"

She breathed a huge sigh, grateful for his understanding. If she didn't look at him, Janelle could picture Tom Wineski as simply the father of a twelve-year-old girl. She could forget the famous face, the perfect body. She wouldn't see the devilish glint in his eye, or remember the way it felt when he touched her. She stared straight ahead, trying to think of him as just another single parent. "It must be even harder for you. You don't even get to do it full-time."

"Yeah, I worry a lot about the kind of influence Elaine's life-style has on Tippy. But then mine wasn't too exemplary until I decided to get serious about parenting."

Janelle forgot her resolve not to look at him. But for once the devilish glint was gone, replaced by a look of regret. The hint of vulnerability was just as appealing. "So," she said, "what made you change?"

Tom shook his head. "The day the judge refused joint custody. I can't tell you what a blow it was. I went home, threw away my little black book, then called my manager and told him to get rid of every public appearance that involved dates.

"Can you tell I'm a changed man? You didn't know me before, but you must have seen the headlines in those supermarket rags. You know, 'Chicago's King and His Harem' or 'Tom Wineski's Wife for a Week and How to Be One.' I ask you, could that be the same man sitting here, enjoying a root-beer float on your back porch?"

"Either a changed man or the sign of a dual personality," Janelle agreed with a smile, remembering her fears earlier in the day. "Actually I *did* wonder how stable you were this afternoon when you suddenly dropped your role and everything about you changed."

"Don't remind me. That has to be one of the dumbest stunts I've ever pulled. The less said about it the better— except that I'm sorry. I just hope you'll give me a chance to prove it."

Janelle wondered if he realized just how suggestive that phrase was. Or was her own imagination just running in overdrive? How could he prove that he was sorry? With an autograph, a bouquet of flowers, a hug and a kiss . . . ?

It was just as well that Tom's voice interrupted that train of thought. "Don't you think it's about time to go to the bus stop?" Without waiting for an answer, he stood up and gathered the glasses, including the one Dan had knocked over.

Janelle followed him into the kitchen, berating herself for her wayward thoughts. She left Tom rinsing the dishes and went to find her purse. She stood in front of the hall closet and lectured herself. She could think more clearly even this short distance away from the charismatic aura he projected. This man was relying on her for help, and all she seemed capable of doing was daydreaming.

You and a million other women.

That thought shut the door on her daydream instantly. There was something about her predictable behavior that rankled. He was only a man, for heaven sakes. A man who was just passing through. A man who thought he could depend on her for help.

She hurried back to the kitchen and urged Tom out the back door. It took a real effort, but she accepted his hand on her back as nothing more than a gesture of graciousness on his part. This time they walked to the detached garage at the far corner of the double lot. Janelle swung the old-fashioned double doors open and Tom waited, closing them for her while she backed her car onto the street.

Tom slipped into the passenger seat but didn't close the door. "Is it all right to leave Dan alone?"

"Of course. He's been staying by himself since he was ten. This is a small town. I'm usually no more than five minutes away. Does Tippy still have a baby-sitter?" Janelle was genuinely surprised.

"Well, there's the housekeeper. She's there most of the time. As far as I know, Tippy's never been alone."

Tom pulled the door shut, and Janelle eased away from the curb for the short trip downtown to the corner bus stop.

"Tom, I remember baby-sitting when I was Tippy's age. And that was in the city. Don't you think you're being a little overprotective?"

"No." His reply was emphatic. "Times have changed, Janelle. For one thing, Tippy doesn't need to earn money baby-sitting or any other way. And insisting on a housekeeper and some adult supervision besides my ex-wife's is the only guarantee I have that she's getting any supervision at all. Elaine forgets she exists half the time."

Janelle could see it was a sensitive subject and dropped it. After all, she was only a casual observer. It was really none of her business.

They had reached the corner and parked in less than three minutes. They sat in strained silence for a while as Tom kept looking at his watch and the occasional sigh betrayed his impatience.

"I suppose you could get out and walk around," Janelle suggested halfheartedly, "but I'm afraid someone might recognize you."

"Yeah, I'm not sure I want Tippy's first sight of Jackson to be filled with screaming autograph hounds."

Janelle tried to suppress her laughter, and it came out as a snort. She gave up and laughed out loud. "Really, Tom, sometimes your ego shows. I don't think even *you* could generate a screaming mob in Jackson at eleven at night." She turned in the seat and faced him squarely, her eyes alight with a challenging mischief.

Tom looked surprised at her frank reply, but replied in good humor. "You didn't have to escape out the bathroom window this afternoon. Those girls were chanting and banging on the door. It was *not* pleasant."

This time her laughter came in short, breathy puffs. "You escaped out the window? I wish I could have seen that."

"Janelle, I think you have the most charming laugh in the tri-state area, but I wish you wouldn't use it on me quite so often. I tell you, it was no laughing matter. I've been in some uncomfortable positions before. But trapped in a small-town motel room with only cable TV for company wasn't my idea of a good time.

"Oh, true hardship, Tom. Did you check to see if the cable showed the adult channel? That would have been diverting."

"I can see I'm not going to get any sympathy from you." He turned away in feigned annoyance and flipped on the radio.

No sympathy from me, Tom, but at least you're not worrying about Tippy anymore.

A loud tap sounded on the driver's side window, just as Tom had settled on the loudest rock station he could find. It startled them both. Tom turned the radio down as Janelle lowered the window. She recognized one of Jackson's five policemen immediately.

"Oh, it *is* you, Janelle. I couldn't figure out what your car was doing parked here with two adults in it. I guess you got company and are waitin' for more yet." As he spoke he bent down lower to get a good look at her passenger.

Janelle angled her body to shield Tom from view. "That's right, Carl. We're just waiting for a friend. She should be on the bus from Chicago."

"Okay then, Nell." Carl spoke automatically, still struggling for a view of her passenger. But the darkness and shadow from the streetlight made a casual identification impossible. The officer gave up and straightened. "The bus is about five minutes late out of Janesville. Be seeing you."

"Thanks, Carl. Tell Myrna I said hi." Janelle rolled up the window promptly and turned to her passenger.

"Well, that's it, Tom. In fifteen minutes he'll have figured out who you are. Then you'll have your crowd. Let's hope the bus doesn't lose any more time."

Tom didn't appear the slightest bit interested in the possibility. "Janelle, do you mean to say that you've never been in this car with an adult male?"

"Don't be silly. It was just Carl's excuse to see who I was with. Probably the only thing that will happen on his beat all night. I have men in the car all the time. My father-in-law, Dan, Ned, my brother-in-law, even an occasional date." Janelle added the last as casually as she could, hoping Tom wouldn't recognize it for the lie it was.

"Must be pretty occasional, Janelle, to generate that much interest." He edged a little closer to her on the seat. "Tell me, Nell." Janelle was certain he used the hated nickname to deliberately tease her. "When was the last time you parked in a car with a man?"

Janelle stared at him a moment, actually trying to remember. Living in Jackson as "Arnie Harper's widow" generated a hands-off message that no man had ever tested. The last time she'd parked with a man was so far back in time that all she could recall was a vague memory. It was nothing to compare with the response generated by simply sitting next to this one.

Janelle was never so glad to see a bus in her life.

Tom forgot his baiting question immediately. They both got out of the car, and Tom moved down to the corner while Janelle waited by the car door. The ungainly vehicle made a noisy stop, and the double doors swung open with a hydraulic whoosh.

Janelle watched one young woman get off the bus and looked for Tom's twelve-year-old daughter. She was surprised that there was more than one passenger stopping in Jackson and even more surprised when the doors swung shut and the bus lumbered on down the street.

With her attention focused on Tom and his daughter, she watched as they walked toward her. The girl was dressed like an adult in an outlandish leather miniskirt. Her hair stood straight up in spikes, and as Tippy passed under the streetlight, Janelle could have sworn the girl's hair was dyed green. As the two approached, she noticed that suddenly Tom looked unbearably tired and the girl sullen and unfriendly.

"Hi, Tippy, welcome to Jackson." Janelle pulled open the car door, not waiting for a response from the girl. She really was a child, Janelle reminded herself. "Here, why don't you sit up front next to your dad?"

Without a word, the trio sorted themselves into seats. Janelle pulled the seat belt around herself and handed Tippy hers. The girl took it and laid it in her lap without fastening it.

A tired, upset child, Janelle added to herself.

She looked across the girl to Tom. "The motel, I presume."

Suddenly the girl came alive. "No way, Dad. I am *not* staying in some crummy motel with you. Not unless I can have my own room so I can watch TV even if you want to go to sleep."

Tom looked apologetically at Janelle. "An old argument, I'm afraid." He addressed his daughter. "Listen, honey. It's late and I can't get another room tonight. I would if I could, but this isn't Chicago, and the desk clerk has gone home by now. It's just for one night."

The girl stuck out her chin. "Forget it, Dad. You'll just have to wake him up."

"How about if Tippy stays in the guest room at my house."

Tom perked up a little at the suggestion, but Tippy became even more adamant. "Dad, I'm not going to stay alone in some strange person's house unless you're there, too." She paused a moment and added, "I know Mom wouldn't approve of it."

If the last was calculated to generate a response, it succeeded. Tom looked over at Janelle, "Do you suppose I could sleep on the couch or somewhere else at your house."

He looked so unlike the macho, arrogant, heart-stopping hero that Janelle couldn't refuse. He was simply a parent, and a rather desperate one at that. "Sure," she replied with a cheer she was far from feeling. Turning on the engine, she headed back home, and a short while later they stood in the kitchen.

Apparently Tippy recognized the limits of her father's tolerance and went to bed without delay. Tom came downstairs a few minutes later and sank into one of the living room chairs.

"God, I'm glad she didn't have time to dress up for this visit." Tom's burst of sarcasm renewed Janelle's faith in his humanity. Only Superman, or Superdad, would have let it go by without comment. "Just her good old miniskirt and the green hair." He continued, "I always think I should hand her a whip and a chair when she wears that outfit. Is it part of the twelve-year-old mentality to dress like you're twenty and act like you're eight?"

Janelle accepted the question for the rhetorical statement it was. Tom Wineski had her complete sympathy. "Tom, if it makes you feel any better, I remember last Easter Dan dressed like an adult and then got into a knockdown fight with his seven-year-old cousin over a game of 'Candyland.'"

As intended, Tom smiled at the picture Janelle drew. "I don't know whether to be relieved that I'm not alone or extend my sympathies to you for being in the same boat."

Janelle wasn't sure what to say next, but opted for diplomacy. "Children can really complicate your life, can't they?"

He looked relieved at her understanding. "Yeah, I don't care how much money and success you have, you can't protect your kids from themselves or from life. They have to grow up, and there's just no easy way to do it.

"I remember when she was going through the 'terrible twos.' Elaine and I almost went nuts. But it was a piece of cake compared to this teenage garbage. Wait, make that preteen garbage. She's not even a teenager yet." He groaned. "I'm not sure I'll survive."

"Oh, come on, Tom. Don't you remember what it was like? You were a teenager once, too. That must be some help. I know it is to me." Of course, Janelle had to admit that she didn't have half the problems Tom did.

"Believe me, Janelle, there's no comparison. The girl cries all the time. She's either hanging all over me or can't stand to have me around. At her age I was in every sport you could name and had energy to spare. She spends all her time in her room. I understand the entire Chicago press corps better than I understand my own daughter."

"Probably because you spend more time with them." Oops, she thought, that wasn't very diplomatic. She hurried on. "What I mean is, you really don't see that much of her on a day-to-day basis, right? She's growing and changing a lot right now. The fact is, she probably doesn't even understand herself half the time."

Tom dismissed the subject with a shrug. They sat quietly, each lost in their own thoughts. Obviously the man was willing to do just about anything for his daughter. Janelle wondered if that wasn't part of the problem.

"Tom, you can sleep in the sitting room half of my bedroom. It closes off into a separate room, and there's a chaise longue there that should work. Come on, you're about ready to drop."

They climbed the stairs slowly. As they walked down the hall to Janelle's room, Tom slipped his arm around her shoulder in a gesture of support. The shared feeling of parents in trouble disappeared as soon as they crossed the bedroom's threshold.

Janelle had never realized quite how sensual her bedroom was. Or maybe it was just that the king-size brass bed dominated the space so completely. She stiffened slightly, and Tom dropped his arm from around her shoulder. Not looking at him, she moved through the open doors to the sitting room, and began pulling sheets from the wooden trunk under the window.

"I hope this chaise won't be too uncomfortable for you. You're at least six inches taller than me. Your feet are bound to hang off the end. I guess you could sleep in my bed." Janelle stopped speaking, stealing a quick glance at Tom to see if he'd noticed she was babbling.

He was leaning against the door frame, considering her last words. He straightened and took the handful of blankets and sheets. "Janelle, I'm going to be just fine here. Now get into your half of the room and go to sleep." With the pile of linens between them, he stretched toward her and kissed her lightly. It was the merest meeting of lips. A simple touching, not much more personal than a handshake. It was over in a second, and while Tom may have meant it as a gesture of reassurance it had a devastating effect on Janelle. She stared at him for a moment, lost in the awakening of a thousand long-dormant fantasies, then moved into her room, sliding the door shut.

Twenty minutes later Janelle lay in her bed listening to the sounds of the house at rest. She'd finally managed to replace the erotic longing with simple restlessness. She punched her pillow, venting a mixture of annoyance and embarrassment.

She wished she could have said something clever and amusing instead of acting like a star-struck teen. But Janelle knew that clever and amusing wasn't her style. She was more of an outraged moralist.

With a groan smothered in the pillow, Janelle squirmed further under the covers and began counting sheep.

It was the raucous sound of birds that woke him. He was used to sirens, trash trucks, even the more subtle sounds of the high-rise ventilation system, but not the combination of sweet and strident birdcalls at 5:30 a.m. The sound roused him as effectively as an alarm clock.

Tom moved his body carefully. Sleeping in a half-sitting position had been more comfortable than he'd expected. Except for an annoying crick in his neck, the rest of his body felt as rested as four hours of sleep would allow.

He wished he could settle back into bed and enjoy the sounds of nature as he drifted back to sleep. It was an empty wish. A slow stretch alleviated the crick. Twisting his neck from side to side dispelled the soreness. The last of the kinks disappeared as he pulled himself into a sitting position.

A noise from outside caught his attention. It was a strange squeaking sound followed by a pause, then a thud. The sound repeated, growing closer and closer, and then faded away. Paper boy on a bicycle, he decided, a bicycle in need of oil. There was another sound in the near distance, and he strained to identify it. A train chugging somewhere, but no cars and not one high altitude roar from an airplane.

He was wide awake now, ready for some coffee and a shower. Maybe he would catch a few winks later in the day, in between teasing Janelle and spending time with Tippy. He rolled off the chaise, stood and stretched and pulled on the clothes that were lying in a heap on the floor.

The only way out of the small sitting area was through Janelle's bedroom, and he slid the door open cautiously, glad that it seemed well oiled and silent. He left it open, afraid to risk sound by closing it again.

The gentleman in him insisted that he walk by without a glance at the sleeping woman. The rake in him couldn't resist just a peek. She was still sound asleep, having pleasant dreams if the slight smile on her lips was any indication. Her hair seemed more red than brown spread across the pillows that propped her up, and she looked like some elegant sleeping beauty waiting for a lover's kiss. He was disappointed that she was wearing some kind of tailored pajamas and not the teddy he'd seen hanging in the bathroom the day before.

As he walked quietly out of the room, Tom considered several other ways of starting the day, none of which centered around tiptoeing down to the kitchen to make coffee before a three-mile run. Under other circumstances, he might have tried to act out those options, but the fact that his daughter and her son were in residence was almost as effective as a cold shower.

He found the coffeepot easily. Fortunately, the machine was one he was familiar with—one of the few modern appliances he'd seen in the kitchen. As the coffee dripped, he went to the front door and collected the paper.

He glanced at the front page before he folded it under his arm. No big news, this was a local paper, a weekly. There wasn't one article on current world problems. The headline story was a tentative listing of activities for the annual Fall Fest, still two months away.

He returned to the rocking chair on the back porch. He checked out the living room and walked through the dining room, but decided it was too nice a morning to be inside. The porch was as comfortable a place as any. Settling in the chair, he drank his first cup of coffee in complete peace. His only company was a trail of ants that had discovered the root-beer puddle left from Dan's spilled glass the night before. Down the street another early riser watched a dog run in the large ball field almost a block from Janelle's house.

He imagined Janelle sitting out here most summer mornings. Was she used to the exceptional peace and quiet? Did she sit here and look around and enjoy the roses spilling over the fence or the sight of the garden filled with ripe tomatoes? He couldn't find a thing amiss in the rural domestic picture her home and yard presented. Tom had to admit that part of the charm was due to the woman herself. She was downright sweet and thoughtful, adjectives he hadn't used in a long time. Not too good at teasing him back, but frank to a fault. Not really maternal as he'd thought earlier; maybe the word was perceptive.

The list of virtues should sound outdated and archaic. Here in this setting they seemed perfectly natural. How content was she here? She seemed financially secure, her son seemed well adjusted, but what kind of social life did she have? By her own admission, not much of one.

It was a lack he wouldn't mind correcting, but now just wasn't the right time, even though the place was pretty appealing. He thought back over the last few years and the new image he'd worked so hard to cultivate. It hadn't been all that hard to give up the old life-style; now he realized that had been because no one had tempted him the way Janelle did.

He remembered the absurd brush of the lips they'd shared last night. He tried to tell himself he'd meant it to be reassuring, but deep down he knew it was a test. Whether a test of him or her, he couldn't say any more than he could say whether they'd passed or failed. All he knew was that sleep had been slow in coming, his body racing with a sexual longing he was hard-pressed to control.

Who would have thought he would be so attracted to a widow from a small town. He shrugged away the irony and concentrated on the paper.

It took ten minutes to read it, including the obituaries. Two folks who lived at the county home had died, as well as the owner of one of the local service stations. As he looked over the listings of cars for sale and the few real estate ads, the door slammed and Dan stumbled out onto the porch with a glass of juice in hand.

At first Tom was surprised to see him so early, then he remembered Janelle's comment last night about Dan's swim meet. A morning person himself, Tom still recognized all the symptoms of a slow riser and didn't say a word until the boy spoke first.

"Got a swim meet today. My ride should be here anytime."

"Well, listen, good luck, Dan. What strokes are you swimming?"

The boy grimaced, obviously trying to get his brain to function. "Don't remember." Suddenly the boy seemed more alert, grabbed the gym bag at his feet and jumped down the steps. "Ride's here. Bye, Tom. See you later."

He watched the car out of sight and returned to the paper. Car prices were reasonable, but the housing prices were really cheap. There was even a service station for sale at Whitewater and Highway 32. That was only a few blocks away. Tom thought about walking down to take a look at it later in the day, just for something to do.

The caffeine had reactivated his system, and he stood and began the stretching exercises that were a normal part of his running routine. He figured he could run back to the motel, shower and drive back over before anyone else was up. He decided to leave Janelle and Tippy a note just in case.

Stepping back into the kitchen, he walked the few feet to the phone he'd used the night before. He remembered the pad of paper and pencil lying nearby.

The phone rang. He grabbed the receiver before the first ring was complete, anxious not to wake Janelle or Tippy. "Hello."

There was no response. It was then he realized that he'd made a grave tactical error.

Finally, the caller spoke. It was a woman. "Is Janelle there?" The voice was hesitant, obviously surprised by the deep masculine voice that greeted her.

Maybe, Tom thought, there was a chance to escape. "Gee, there's no one here by that name—"

The surprise disappeared instantly along with the hesitation. "Young man, this is no wrong number. I have my daughter-in-law's number programmed into this fancy phone. I know it dialed right."

Whoa boy, Tom thought, what a great first impression this is. Before he could plan a graceful escape she continued, her tone now conversational, almost businesslike. "Is she up yet? I thought she would be about ready to drive Dan over to the swim meet."

"Dan rode with someone else, Mrs. Harper. Janelle's still asleep. Do you want me to wake her up? She was up pretty late last night—" Tom stopped short.

"You better quit right there, young man. You're only digging yourself in deeper." He hoped that was humor he heard in her voice. "You tell Nell that I'll call later. I just wanted to talk to her about dinner on Sunday. I guess I'll be seeing you there. Bye."

He turned away from the phone, completely forgetting the note he'd planned to leave. Another cup of coffee was the least he needed to soothe his jangled nerves.

Janelle stood in the doorway. Her hair was a jumble of sleep-wrestled curls. Her robe, a shiny, satin, tailored thing in white hung open as though she'd thrown it on in a hurry. It didn't matter. The pink cotton pajamas he'd noted earlier were in place and as nonrevealing as any bathrobe. Her feet were bare. She stood leaning against the door frame, and Tom wondered if she were about to go to sleep again.

He poured a cup of coffee and handed it to her, then leaned against the counter and watched. Slowly, unconsciously, his inclination to remain uninvolved faded.

Still silent, she accepted it and took a cautious sip. She smiled and then took a healthier swallow. Tom watched with amusement, then appreciation as her body responded to the caffeine. First a deep breath that expanded her chest and pushed her firm, full breasts against the thin cotton fabric. Then she opened her eyes and tried to absorb her surroundings. Next she pulled her body away from the door frame and stretched up on her toes as if encouraging the caffeine to settle in every nook and cranny. With a final sigh she looked at Tom and smiled.

This woman is like a stick of dynamite. Tom tried to remember why his first impression had been so uncomplimentary. It must have been the clothes. Yet the pajamas weren't any more seductive. Maybe it was the hair. Just one of the little clues that hinted at a sensual nature too long ignored. The painted toenails, the peach teddy, the big brass bed and now that wonderful length of hair, falling in soft curls over her shoulders. It framed her face and enhanced those lovely eyes and that very kissable mouth. It even made the robe look good. The shiny satin reflected the red highlights of her hair, turning the material around her face a soft pink.

He was sure she didn't mean to look seductive. Her behavior last night had told him quite clearly that she wasn't interested. And after their disastrous introduction, he wasn't about to make a move without a clear-cut signal from her.

Right now the signals were unconscious. He was sure of that. Well, almost sure. Maybe he would move just a little closer and test her response.

Moving away from the counter, he took a step to close the distance between them. She smiled again and took a step closer and Tom allowed himself to feel a little encouraged. His own smile broadened as she stepped still closer. Just as he was about to pull her against him, she stepped around him and grabbed the coffeepot.

Oh my God, what am I doing? I almost walked right into his arms! That's what happens when you're awakened from your dreams only to come face-to-face with the star of them. It took both her shaking hands to balance the pot enough to pour her second cup of coffee. She took a long swallow and organized her thoughts before she turned to face Tom again.

He was standing against the opposite counter by the phone, looking just a little disconcerted. With a quiet sigh of relief, Janelle gave him her best impersonal smile.

"So, I guess that was Irene, my mother-in-law, on the phone?"

"Listen, I'm really sorry; I didn't think before I answered it. I hope it won't be a problem for you."

That's it, Janelle thought. Get him on the defensive and he won't notice how flustered you are. Now ask about Tippy and he'll forget all about the way you almost threw yourself at him. "Do you think Tippy will sleep in? I guess last night was pretty hard on her."

Tom shrugged his shoulders and closed the few feet between them. Just as Janelle was beginning to panic, he reached around her and picked up his coffee cup. He turned and looked at her blandly. She stepped away quickly and headed for her usual spot at the breakfast table.

"I don't know what she'll do, Janelle. She might sleep all day, and she might be down here in five minutes. We'll know when she shows up. In the meantime, here's the paper and I'm off for the motel. I'll take a shower there, then bring the car back and park it in your garage."

Before Janelle could answer, Tom was out the door. Before it slammed, he stuck his head back in. "If Tippy wakes up sooner than later, just try and keep her from panic. I'll be back pretty quickly." With a smile and a wink he was gone. Janelle watched as he jumped off the porch steps and started down the street.

So much for seduction before seven. Janelle pulled the paper close and turned to the classified ads, hoping for at least one or two good estate sales to take her mind off her houseguest—make that houseguests. She tried to concentrate on the ads and pushed the picture of Tom Wineski and his twinkling eyes from her mind. It was harder to dispel the restlessness his presence had generated, and she pretended it was the first shot of caffeine that caused the breathlessness she was still trying to control.

Pulling out the map she kept stashed in the basket at the side of the table, she checked the location of the two sales listed. She didn't know what Tom's plans were. What's more, she insisted to herself, she didn't care. Janelle Harper was escaping from this madhouse and heading to Watertown to check out the depression glass mentioned in the estate sale ad.

Placing her mug in the sink, Janelle headed out of the kitchen. If she showered and changed quickly, she would be ready to leave just as Tom returned. She would imitate his breezy style and even started practicing a few exit lines as she headed for the stairs.

She had her foot on the first step when the phone rang. Abandoning her casual pace, she raced back to the kitchen and answered the phone before the second ring. The caller spoke before Janelle even said hello. It had to be Kathy. That was one sister-in-law who never wasted time on greetings.

"Hey, Nell, sorry to get you out of bed so early. But I couldn't wait another minute. Tell me. What's it like to spend the night with Tom Wineski?"

Four

Kathy's phone call was just the beginning. Janelle spent ten minutes answering Kathy's questions about her surprise houseguest, but cut her sister-in-law off as Tippy came stumbling down the steps in search of her father. The girl looked tired, then frightened when Janelle told her that Tom had gone to the motel for a shower and a change of clothes. With maternal concern, Janelle motioned Tippy to the table and poured her a glass of juice. Janelle was about to join her when the doorbell rang.

It didn't stop. First the policeman from the night before stopped by to see if her guest had arrived safely. He was followed by a neighbor from across the street who brought an offering of beans from his garden. Janelle had more than enough beans from her own harvest, but she accepted his with good grace and ignored his angling for an invitation inside.

It took Tom only an hour to return, but by then, two more neighbors had stopped by and a couple of girls rode their bikes up and down the street in anxious anticipation.

When they caught sight of Tom's old Porsche, they screamed at the top of their lungs. Whether they intended to or not, they passed a signal to the rest of the neighborhood. Within minutes, people were hurrying down the sidewalk, and the street in front of Janelle's house was crowded with double-parked cars.

At least Tom knew how to handle the situation. Charging through the house, he gave Tippy a quick hello and grabbed the pad and pencil by the phone. The phone began to ring again and Tom reached over, pulling the plug. He glanced at Janelle, his expression a mix of apology and resignation, and headed for the front porch and the growing crowd of fans.

Janelle followed him, wanting to help, but not sure how to control the increasingly excited crowd. Fortunately, the police arrived just as Tom opened the door. While they weren't trained in crowd control, the officers were on a first-name basis with almost everyone and were able to exert a calming influence.

With the pressure off, or at least focused on Tom, Janelle headed back to the kitchen, turning her attention to Tippy, who still sat at the kitchen table. Janelle poured herself a cup of coffee and sat down across the table from the young girl.

She waited a moment, hoping Tippy would say something. Eyes the same color as Tom's focused on her. "You know, it was a dumb idea for me to come here. I should have just waited for Daddy to come home."

For an instant, Janelle was reminded of Tom again, but not in the way Tippy spoke or what she said. She remembered his comments about the difficulty of single parenting, the challenge of the teenage years. The whole process was made even more complex by the lack of privacy that came with fame. She felt a rush of sympathy for both parent and child caught in such a difficult situation.

Dan's arrival ended any attempt at further conversation. Janelle tried to introduce any number of suitable topics for the two youngsters to talk about, but neither showed the slightest interest. They seemed to regard each other as alien life-forms. The girl looked as though smiling was a lost art, and all that interested Dan was how many pieces of syrupy French toast he could stuff into his mouth at once.

Janelle sipped her coffee and tried not to let her annoyance show. "I know there's no way we can really call this a typical Saturday, Dan." Janelle paused until her son turned his full attention to her. "I mean, how often do we have two houseguests?" She directed a smile at Tippy, grateful that the child couldn't read her thoughts. "Why don't the two of you go up to the pool, the way you always do on Saturday. I heard from Kathy that DC and his band are going to be practicing for the outdoor dance. What do you think?"

"You mean I can go to the dance?"

Janelle shook her head. Dan's powers of deduction constantly amazed her. "Dan, that is not what I said. DC practices in that field right next to the pool. If you go up to swim, you'll get to hear them, too. We both know that you have to be fourteen to go to the dance, and everyone in this town knows you're twelve."

"But, Mom, that doesn't matter. I keep telling you all the kids sneak in and no one cares."

"The answer is no, Dan. Now, how about the two of you going to the pool?"

Dan was about to press the issue when Tippy spoke up. "Sounds just like my Dad." She didn't appear to be addressing anyone in particular. "I can't do anything that's any fun when I'm with him."

Tippy turned her attention to Janelle. "How come you don't have air conditioning? It's really hot here. I'd go swimming, but I didn't bring my bikini with me."

She gave Janelle a smirk that begged for retribution. Instead, Janelle attempted a genuine smile in return, ignoring the crack about air conditioning. "Actually, I have some extra suits for the swim team. They changed styles last year, and I still have about five of the old ones on hand. One of them is sure to fit you."

It took some scrambling, but thirty minutes later Janelle waved goodbye as the two began the six block walk to the community pool. She almost whooped out loud at her success. They weren't exactly talking to each other—they weren't even walking together—but Janelle was willing to bet money that by dinnertime they would forget their initial dislike.

That left only one Wineski to cope with. Why did he have to meet his fan club on her front porch? It wouldn't take long for the whole town to link their names. With a resigned shrug, she decided the best way to handle Tom was to leave him on his own. If she wasn't around, people would be less inclined to speculate on their relationship.

She finished tidying the kitchen, leaving a healthy serving of French toast for Tom's brunch. Then she walked quietly toward the stairs, fully intending to slip past the front entry and upstairs to make the beds. It all seemed so stupid—she was sneaking around in her own house.

The front door was wide open, with the screen door closed to keep out the summer bugs. Tom's broad shoulders blocked most of the light, as well as the view into the house.

"Oh, come on, Tom."

Janelle paused on the steps. She recognized the voice of the one-man news team at the local radio station. "You *are* staying at her house and you *did* spend the night. You can't be serious when you say there's nothing between you."

Janelle turned slowly on the stairs, resentment boiling up inside her. If she had had a bucket handy she would have drowned the boor. Instead she listened for Tom's response, more than willing to include him in her anger.

"I can tell you one thing, buddy. I didn't come here to give interviews. Now, if you don't want an autograph, why don't you get out of the way and let me talk to the people who do. You can call my manager and try to schedule an interview like the rest of the press."

The crowd didn't seem to mind Tom's arrogance and shouted its approval. Janelle waited a moment longer for

Tom to explain their nonrelationship. But his voice was a low-key rumble as he spoke to fans. He seemed to consider the subject closed, and Janelle resisted the urge to say something herself. The reporter slipped to the back of the crowd, hanging on the fringe, obviously hoping that Tom's casual remarks would give him some scoop.

Maybe it would be in her best interest to rescue him from the group outside. But how? After a moment's consideration, Janelle rejected the idea. He was the expert. If he wanted to get rid of them, he probably had fifteen different techniques. This adulation was what it was all about.

With a snort of disgust, Janelle turned her attention to Dan's bedroom. The bed was made, after a fashion, but a week's worth of dirty clothes littered the floor, and Janelle knew that if she didn't gather them and wash them herself, he would be wearing his bathing suit for the rest of the summer.

Tippy's bed wasn't made. Green coloring stained the pillow cover, and Janelle slipped the case off and replaced it with another. She'd always wondered why pillowcases came in twos.

Tom had folded his sheets and neatly stacked them on top of the chaise longue. Janelle had to struggle not to picture Tom stretched out on it, the sheets twisted around his night-shadowed body.

She stowed the pillow back in the wooden trunk and added his sheets to the pile of dirty clothing. There was no way he was staying another night. She worked her way carefully down the steps with the full basket and tried to ignore the breathless, high-pitched giggles coming from the front porch.

"Aw, please, Tom," the girlish voice wheedled, "just a little piece of your shirt. I'd love to have something to remember you by."

I could probably make a fortune selling these sheets, Janelle thought, pausing once again to hear Tom's response.

"Listen, sweet stuff, this is the only shirt I have with me. But if you go home and get a camera, I'll get someone to take a picture of us. Wouldn't that be a better keepsake?"

King was back.

Picking up her pace once again, Janelle grabbed the dirty dish towels from the kitchen and headed to the basement to stuff a load of wash in the machine. The basement was damp and cool and just a little musty—not one of Janelle's favorite places. But today she seriously considered hiding down there until the furor died down.

What a miserable way to spend the weekend. She compared her initial confrontation with King to the Tom Wineski who'd shared root-beer floats on the back porch and gently kissed her good-night. Why did he even bother with that awful character?

A smile dimpled her cheeks as she remembered that good-night kiss. Then she recalled what was going on on her front porch and sobered at the thought.

She pursed her lips and pulled the smile off, but the sensuous memory of his lips on hers lingered. It was incredible that such a simple gesture of affection could leave her so flustered, and feeling that she desperately wanted more.

With a sigh of disappointment, Janelle walked slowly up the basement steps and back into the kitchen, trying to think of a few other chores that would keep her occupied and distract her from the commotion on the front porch.

That was the trouble with Saturdays, she decided. There just wasn't enough to do. Usually she welcomed the chance to sit on the porch and read or do a little sewing, but today both those activities required more concentration than she was able to muster.

Her mind was elsewhere. Only to herself would she even half admit that Tom Wineski fascinated her. Not because he was a celebrity. Not because he drove a neat car or was rich. The fact was that he was the first man in five years who'd elicited any kind of emotional response from her. Never mind that half that response was active annoyance, if not downright dislike. There was definitely an attraction. And when he wasn't playing some phony Hollywood role, he was close to irresistible.

She headed toward the front door again with a cold soda in hand. It was hot and humid and the temperature was still climbing. If Tom wasn't hungry, he was surely thirsty. The crowd was more orderly now, but not much smaller. They clustered around the front porch, watching Tom intently as they waited their turns for a picture or an autograph. Pushing the door open, she tapped him on the shoulder and held out the soda can.

"Come on out, Janelle. I'm sure these folks would love to have a picture of you, too." Despite her violent headshake, he pulled her by the hand that held the can until she stood next to him.

"Hey, King," a voice called from the rear of the crowd, "is Janelle gonna take Mrs. Murphy's place."

"It would be hard to replace Murphy, wouldn't it?" The crowd agreed with a cheer. "There aren't too many sixty-year-old women with her spunk.

"She was a real nuisance at first, but now she's about the only bright spot in King's life. Fridays wouldn't be the same without her pot roast."

"Don't you get tired of it?" It was the reporter still lurking on the fringe who called out the question.

Janelle listened, trapped in the circle of Tom's arm. She pulled away a little, wanting to distance herself from the scene, but Tom held firm. She glared up at him, but the effect was lost as she squinted into the sun. He pulled her a little closer, but the chemistry had faded moments ago. It was Tom she was attracted to, not King. She listened to the tale of Mrs. Murphy in amazement. These people, Tom included, were talking about King as if he were a real person. Couldn't they distinguish between TV and reality?

"Now, why don't you take a picture of the two of us and call it a day."

There were several answering clicks, but a chorus of disapproval drowned them out. Taking advantage of the noise, Janelle urgently pulled herself out of his hold and moved toward the door so he had to turn his back to the crowd. "Tom, I just came out to bring you a pop, not to be part of the show. Do you want this or not?"

She held out the can and prepared to exit.

"Thanks, Nell, but I can't drink that brand. I promote their competitor, and it's in the contract that I can't drink that stuff in public. Do you have—"

It was the last straw. Without waiting for him to complete the sentence, she swept into the house. The screen door banged behind her. Let the man die of thirst. She wasn't going to join all those other fools who catered to his whims. Anger surged through her, anger at herself, anger at Tom Wineski. She was as close to a temper tantrum as she ever got.

She made a beeline through the house from front to back. Pulling a basket off a hook by the back door, she headed out to the garden.

It was small by Jackson standards, taking up only a fraction of the backyard. From the house it appeared to be a riot of vines and bushes with patches of color blooming in the August sun. Up close, the garden was meticulously tended, weeded and fertilized. Several varieties of tomatoes hung heavy on the bushes that marked the back boundary of Janelle's property. They were just ripe enough to harvest for Sunday's Harper family dinner. She'd planned to wait until tomorrow so the vegetables would be as fresh as possible, but right now she needed the calm that working in the garden generated.

She stood on the back porch a moment, eyeing the garden from the distance, willing the surge of anger to dissipate. The mélange of greens were easily separated by her experienced eye, and she walked down the steps, already losing herself in the garden's color and smell.

A glance at the beans, a more careful inspection of the squash, and a sniff of the pungent dill, and she was at the back of the plot. Eyeing the rest of the vegetables, Janelle turned her attention to the hedge of tomato bushes. She pulled on the gloves that always sat in the bottom of her basket and pulled out the plastic mat. Settling the mat in the dirt, Janelle dropped to her knees, working on the underside of the bush first. She culled the closest vines, pulling the ripe fruit off and dropping the cherry tomatoes gently into the basket.

Soon the smell of the slightly bruised tomatoes filled her senses, and she was flooded with the feelings that summed up everything she loved about living in Jackson. Life was close to the earth, even here in town. Even a relative newcomer such as Janelle learned that the land was the measure for everything else, putting everything in perspective. It didn't take long for her anger to dissolve, though Janelle wasn't really conscious of time passing.

She pulled a few tomatoes and let thoughts run randomly through her mind. She hated that nickname, and was certain she'd made that clear from the moment they met.

She paused at the thought, realizing she didn't mind the name so much when it came from everyone else.

She pulled a few more tomatoes, wondering why Tom even bothered with King when his own personality was much more appealing?

For the first time she realized how much his fame limited his life. The sun, the earth, peace and quiet, they were the only real essentials. Why bother with the rest when it kept you from the basics?

Janelle suddenly saw things very clearly. Leaning back on her heels to stretch her back muscles, she eyed the half-full basket, trying to estimate how many more she would need. Then she smiled. She would pick the rest tomorrow. Tom must be thirsty. She could easily pour his pop into a glass so no one would know what brand it was. She stood up and hurried back to the kitchen. Tossing a perfect cherry tomato into her mouth, she made a mental list of things that would introduce Tom Wineski to the real world.

Two rocking chairs creaked in companionable counterpoint. The porch was dark and the kitchen lights were out.

Tom stared out onto the night-darkened street. There wasn't a soul in sight and it was wonderful.

He took a swallow of the beer that was the last of his dinner and smiled at Janelle. "I appreciated that glass of soda this afternoon, it was the only thing between me and complete dehydration."

Janelle smiled back. "I figured you could pretend it was whatever brand you're promoting this week. How would they know?"

He nodded and saluted her with his beer glass. "Sorry about making such a fuss over the can, but there were all those darn cameras around. I hope the glass wasn't part of an heirloom set. I have no idea what happened to it."

"I even thought of that. I knew we'd never see it again, so I used one of the odd ones I had laying around."

With a nod he drained his glass and resumed his casual rocking. Despite, or maybe because of the emotionally draining day, he felt restless, energized. He thought about running a few miles, then discarded the idea. After the amount he'd eaten at dinner, he wouldn't be able to run for hours.

"You know, I don't think I've ever had a meal that was completely homegrown before. Dan said your father-in-law even caught the fish." It'd been years since he'd had fried fish. But it had been better than anything he could remember. To hell with the cholesterol.

"Sure did, bluegills on Lake Ripley at six this morning. He and my brother-in-law, Ned, go out most Saturday mornings. Sometimes Dan goes, too, if he doesn't have a swim meet or something."

Tom watched her in the darkness. He couldn't see her face, but she sounded awfully pleased with herself. He smiled and played the game. "And the vegetables were all from your garden?"

"Sure were, even the berries, though they'd been frozen. That was good shortcake, if I do say so myself."

"Sure was," he mimicked, and set his chair to rocking in time with hers. He was beginning to get the message. "I'd say that was one of the best meals I've ever eaten, and I've eaten at a lot of fine restaurants.''

Janelle kept on rocking and turned her head to look at him, her eyes watching him suspiciously. ''Are you teasing me?''

His voice was a study in innocence. ''Who, me? No way. It *was* one of the best meals I've ever had. I guess there's something about homegrown food that adds a flavor you don't find anywhere else. Somehow I think that's the real message you wanted me to get.''

''Was I that obvious?'' Embarrassment robbed her face of its smile. ''I guess people are always trying to impress you with something. I just thought...''

She was right, but for the first time in years, Tom *was* impressed. He reached across the table and laid his hand over hers. ''Janelle...''

The slap of sneakered feet against the sidewalk brought both rockers to an abrupt halt.

''Mom! Mom!'' Dan shouted as he and Tippy rounded the corner and headed for the steps. They both stopped short as they spotted the two adults on the porch.

''How come you're sitting in the dark?'' He looked from one to the other, as if craving a little peace and quiet was downright strange. ''Never mind. Can Tippy and I ride out to the farm with Jason and Janet?'' He turned his attention to Tom. ''They're my cousins.'' And then back to his mother. ''Grandma got *Aliens* today, and she said we could watch it and spend the night. That way we can go swimming out there tomorrow, and we'll be there when you all come to dinner.''

Janelle didn't hesitate. ''It's okay with me, Son, but I think Tippy should check with her Dad, too.'' The three turned to Tom as Tippy spoke.

''Well, Daddy.'' Her insolent tone dared her father to refuse.

With an exasperated glance at Tippy, Dan interrupted, ''Please, Tom. Tippy told me that you've never let her stay over with anyone before, but we stay at Grandma's all the time. There's this neat old garage she turned into a play-house for us. We have sleeping bags and air mattresses. There'll be plenty of people around to watch us."

It sounded innocent enough. Good grief, if there was any place he should feel comfortable allowing Tippy a little independence, this town would be it. "I suppose there has to be a first time." He looked at Janelle, who nodded in agreement. He was weakening.

The two young faces brightened instantly and grew serious again as Tom continued speaking. "But, Tippy, I thought you hated those scary science-fiction flicks?"

"I don't know where you got that idea. I *am* almost thirteen." Her obvious embarrassment belied her response.

"It doesn't matter, Tom," Dan volunteered. "I've seen it before. And I already told her that I'd tell her before all the gross parts so she could hide her eyes."

Tom nodded his understanding and grudging acceptance just as a pickup with a slightly damaged muffler rumbled to a stop at the curb.

The cab was already filled with three teenagers and Dan and Tippy hopped into the truck bed where two others called to them.

Tom jumped out of his seat as the truck departed. He turned and looked at Janelle. "I'm not sure that was such a good idea. Do you think they've been drinking?"

Janelle shook her head. "Those are all my nieces and nephews, and I can guarantee they won't touch a beer until they get to the farm. The older ones will probably have one, but my in-laws will keep a close eye on the younger kids."

"I guess that's some consolation. I'd be a fool if I thought that Tippy hasn't been exposed to drugs and alcohol in Chicago." Still, he would have felt better if he'd met the senior Harpers or had a chance to size up the cousins before they took off in a cloud of dust. He would have his chance tomorrow. Besides, it wasn't as if Tippy was going to be a permanent fixture around here, though he could get used to this. He turned his back to Janelle and watched the night sky. This afternoon Jackson had been just another public appearance. But now, with the crowd gone, the evening was working the same magic it had last night. He was just a man, sitting with a woman, enjoying the evening air.

It was incredibly quiet and Tippy was his only worry. Just the way it should be. He turned once again to face Janelle and leaned gingerly against the loose railing.

He shook his head. "It didn't take those two long to work out their differences. I wish all the world's problems could be solved by a long afternoon at the pool."

The rocking stopped as Janelle considered his statement, taking it more seriously than he intended. "Have you ever noticed how much more readily kids drop their defenses. All they really need is to find common ground. Dan told me she's a great diver. He's been looking for someone to give him pointers all summer. And did you notice her hair? That pool water will take the color out of anything. Once that happened, Tippy looked like everyone else and she fit right in."

Janelle stood up and leaned against the railing that ran perpendicularly to the one supporting Tom. He sensed her concentration in the way she measured her words. He gave her his full attention. It wasn't hard. Her hair, pulled back by a barrette at the crown, fell in soft waves to just below her shoulders. She wore a pretty sundress, loose fitting, of a gauzy material that revealed as much as it concealed. She looked sweet, young and very sexy.

"...So if phoniness is the problem, how come you slip into that King character so easily. I mean, Tom, the real you is so much nicer."

He may not have heard the whole speech, but he got the message. The real me? Is that who she saw? He'd spent so much time projecting an image of one kind or another, he was surprised anyone could even find the real Tom. In the split second it took for the thought to flash through his mind, he realized that in twenty-four hours Janelle had come closer to knowing the real Tom Wineski than any other woman ever had. The confusion of their first encounter had stripped away the facades, and for a few minutes he'd faced her with no pretense or protection. It made him nervous. He didn't know Janelle well enough to trust her with that kind of power. He was attracted to her, that much he was sure of, but attraction and trust had very little in common.

He thought about his answer, weighing his words carefully. He wanted her to understand why he had to hide. "Some days, hiding behind 'King' is all the privacy I can get. On a day like today, I do it on purpose. It's a kind of self-protection." Enough baring the soul, he thought. "Besides, it's King these people want to see. Tom Wineski means nothing to them."

She tilted her head to one side, considering his explanation. "I understand what you're saying, but I don't see how anyone could prefer that macho creep to you."

Her sincerity touched him, and he wondered if she knew precisely how much she was telling him. Was she as genuine as she sounded or was she hiding, too? "Janelle, look at it this way. King is part of their fantasy world. And in our fantasies, we tolerate all kinds of things that are unacceptable in real life."

Janelle shook her head, not fully accepting his explanation. He tried another tack, anxious to prove his point. "It's like living a fantasy, even if it's only for a few minutes. Look, how about if I use the King approach on you. You can tell me if he's the answer to all your dreams, or if you'd rather sit on the porch with Tom Wineski."

Folding her arms across her chest, Janelle laughed and shook her head. "I already know the answer. Besides, I've had one run-in with King and once was enough."

Tom dispelled that first meeting with a wave of his hand. "That doesn't count. That was reality for you, and damned frightening if I read your reaction correctly. The point is, this is make-believe, the embodiment of all your wildest dreams." His voice softened as he straightened and moved from the railing. "Just pretend."

Taking only a second to get into character, he moved closer to her. She watched him with a mix of amusement and caution, as if she could sense the change in his personality.

He used his eyes to convince her that Tom Wineski was gone, and it was Janelle Harper and Chicago's King alone on her back porch. Tom knew it was the eyes that made King. They were hard and narrowed, always on the alert for the slightest weakness in the people around him, whether they be friend, foe or lover. The eyes never wavered, and he'd perfected a stare that could intimidate even the most stouthearted.

He put a hand on either side of the railing supporting Janelle. The wood still retained a trace of the day's heat, but it wasn't as warm as Janelle's body. He stood close to her, so close he could see the blue of her eyes deepen and overshadow the hazel. A fraction closer and he would feel her breasts press into his chest. As he trapped her against the porch rail, he watched her smile fade and heard her breath quicken. He smiled King's too cynical half smile.

"Seems to me we didn't quite finish our business in the kitchen yesterday. I've been thinking about it all day, wondering what it would feel like to taste that smile you've been throwing out to everyone but me. Come on." He cupped her chin with his hand and teased her lips with his thumb. "How about just a little smile. It'll make this all the sweeter."

She smiled, but he knew the smile was for Tom. It was sweet and full of good humor, and it was all he could do not to grin back.

"Not bad. Wish I thought you were smiling at me." The smile faded a little and she opened her mouth to respond. King took immediate advantage of the motion. He lowered his head and tasted her mouth with his tongue without preliminaries. King gathered her close, using the persuasive powers of his body, as well as his lips. It was the blatantly physical approach that King used on all his conquests and, according to the script, at any moment Janelle would relax against him and respond.

Tom felt her shudder, a sort of reflex action, whether of rejection or surrender, he wasn't sure. But her body was stiff against his. She hadn't melted into his embrace. She hadn't enjoyed it. As he ended the kiss, he felt her body begin to relax and realized that King's approach didn't suit her at all. Janelle Harper was made for gentle wooing, for soft moonlit kisses, and a slow, languorous seduction that would be all the more potent for the anticipation involved.

Opening his eyes for a moment, he gave Janelle a grin that was all Tom Wineski. She smiled in return, and he kissed the corners of her mouth and the bow of her lips. He felt her smile on his lips and once again pulled her close, not demanding, but with a gentleness that brought her all the closer, as if seeking his touch.

She turned her head slightly and he trailed his kisses down her cheek and neck. He returned his lips to her mouth, this time lost in the sweet, soft feel of her. She parted her lips slightly in invitation, and he used his tongue in a gentle sweep that increased the growing intimacy. Longing grew until it escaped the boundaries of their kiss. He held her close while he memorized the feel of her body so perfectly fitted against him. A sense of belonging that was the foundation of sensual excitement kept them clasped together, their mouths communicating feelings more complex than thoughts.

Somewhere in the waves of desire, Tom's brain deciphered the truth. One kiss would never be enough. With that promise in mind, he drew back slightly, ending the kiss in a long, slow parting that softened the disappointment. They stood a moment, staring at each other, acknowledging the power they'd unleashed.

Tom watched Janelle through a haze of longing. It would be so easy to kiss her again, to draw her further into the passion that lay just a breath away. He hesitated, torn between his own needs and what was right for Janelle, for them.

While he still debated, the magic of the moment was lost. Janelle moved out of his arms and stood beside him, looking out into the yard. She was close to him, and he put his arm around her shoulder in the same companionable gesture he'd used the night before, but the effect wasn't the same. All he could think of was how much he wanted to pull her to him and lose himself again in her eyes and lips.

Janelle cleared her throat and Tom eased his hold. "I guess it's time for you to head back to the motel."

Tom could almost convince himself there was a wealth of disappointment in her words.

"You're right ... I guess." He acknowledged to himself what Janelle already knew—that a night at the Rooster's Rest would do more for her reputation than anything else.

The floorboards creaked as Janelle walked to the back door. Before opening the screen door, she turned. "I'll see you at the farm tomorrow. You have the directions, right?"

Nodding, he patted his shirt pocket. "Right here."

"Well, good night then." She turned abruptly and pulled the door open.

"Janelle." At Tom's call, she looked over her shoulder. "You never did give me your verdict on the kisses."

She smiled a little. "Oh, yes." She considered a moment and her smile grew wider. He dreaded the thought that she might have preferred King.

Her smile was just a breath away from laughter. "You know, I'm not sure." She slipped through the door and turned and looked at him through the screen. "I think—" she paused to consider "—yes, I think maybe we should try it again sometime."

Five

When the Porsche purred to a stop behind the line of pickups and aging sedans on the farm driveway, the whole Harper clan turned up to welcome their guest. They waited with shuffling impatience on the front porch while Janelle hurried out to the car.

She shaded her eyes from the sun and wiped her other hand on her apron. This was probably the sum total of time they would have alone together all day. It was going to be hard to make anything of it with the entire family watching from fifty yards away. She tried to squelch the disappointment. Instead she concentrated on how good Tom looked. His light blue polo shirt fit like a second skin and the jeans he had on were just as snug. It was the same outfit he'd worn yesterday, but she hadn't fully absorbed how sexy he looked in it. She tried to imagine him in a tux, or a bathing suit or maybe nothing at all.

"Hi." She stopped, a little breathless from the run down the driveway and the excitement. She stood before him, smiling an unmistakable welcome.

"Good morning." He smiled too, and leaned against the car, folding his arms. "Nothing I'd like better than to kiss you right here, but I hadn't counted on the audience."

"Oh, right. The audience." Janelle glanced back at the porch and then turned to Tom once again. She kept right on smiling even though she was feeling that peculiar weak-kneed sensation again. Actually, she was getting used to the feeling. Next would come the overwhelming need to touch him.

She slipped her arm through his, relishing the contact, and escorted him up the drive. "It's going to be that kind of day. No one ever comes to these things to be alone together." She laughed out loud at the thought.

"I wish you'd told me that last night." He stopped, holding her back for a moment. "Or were you thinking there's safety in numbers?" The look he gave her was challenging, though framed with a smile.

"Mmm, maybe." She gave him a tug, acknowledging to herself that even in the heart of her family, she wasn't safe from his sensual pull. "Come on, it's too late to back out now."

The introductions were one-sided, since everyone knew who Tom was. Janelle was glad she hadn't wasted any energy on worrying about whether he would fit in. He'd left King behind and treated everyone as though he'd known them for years.

The adults spent most of the time before dinner talking football. The preseason was about to begin and the youngest Harper worked for the Green Bay Packers. It would have been the dominant topic anyway. Tom's presence and his wealth of anecdotes about his football days added spice to the usual mix of conversation, and through it all, Tom treated Janelle with a casual affection that set her apart, but didn't single her out. Janelle relaxed enough to enjoy the interaction. It was turning out to be a perfect afternoon.

Tom was sitting on the arm of Janelle's chair and took a swallow from the bottle of beer someone had handed him.

She watched him laugh and admitted to herself that her feelings for him had changed.

Before "the kiss," Janelle could pretend that all she wanted from Tom was simple friendship. Despite their different life-styles, they shared a lot of the same values and, as single parents, a lot of the same problems. It was a good basis for friendship. But afterward she would have been a fool to deny that she wanted more. She was embarrassed to admit, even to herself, that she was like all the other women who'd crowded around her porch on Saturday. She sat now and watched him as he talked about point spreads with her father-in-law. His arm lay across the back of her chair, and if she leaned back, she could rest her head there and feel his pulse quicken against her neck. Instead she sat up straight and dreamed impossible dreams woven with sunlit kisses and the moonlit dance of love.

All the camaraderie came to an abrupt halt when Katherine and Rod arrived. Tom remembered his attorney was the real reason for his visit to Jackson, and his good humor vanished. His smile was perfunctory, and the look he gave Janelle was a mix of anxiety and regret.

He was closeted with Katherine in the farm office for an hour. During that time Tippy became more and more apprehensive and no one could cajole her out of her ill humor. Finally they left her alone.

Janelle helped in the kitchen, but didn't take part in the conversation. Guilt was an effective antidote for any infatuation—and Janelle definitely felt guilty. The man was planning a new custody fight over his child, and all she could worry about was whether they would have a moment alone before he left.

Everyone gathered on the front porch to send off a solemn Tom and a sullen Tippy. Janelle stood on the fringe of the family group, wishing she could kiss away all his worries and anxieties. Her eyes filled with tears as Tom stopped before her. His smile dried her eyes and she smiled back tentatively.

The ominous rumble of thunder and the porch full of people faded into an amorphous background. Tom pulled her into an embrace that was a mix of passion and gratitude. Resting her cheek on his chest, she felt his heart beating steadily, each pulse communicating longing, need, regret. A hundred jumbled messages were embodied in that one furious embrace.

Her own thoughts weren't much more orderly and instead of words, she reached up to kiss his cheek and hug him just one more time. The tears were gone, but she bit her lip to keep it from trembling.

A flash of lightning close by hurried the rest of the farewells. All the Harpers shouted their goodbyes and begged for a return visit. Janelle joined in, knowing it was a futile wish.

By the middle of the next week, the whole weekend seemed like a fantasy. Kids still stopped by to ask for an autograph and cars passed the house very slowly, but there was nothing else to mark the time when the people of Jackson could boast: "Tom Wineski slept here."

Sitting in the kitchen, nursing her second cup of coffee, Janelle listened to the final drips of summer rain echo on the metal porch roof. The hollow sounds were resonant with lonely days and empty nights. Janelle admitted that as much as she wanted more, she and Tom would never get beyond the beginning. He lived in Chicago and she was in Jackson, and lots more than two hours separated them. When and why would he ever come to Jackson again? Of course, she could always go to Chicago. But if she'd learned one thing over the weekend it was that people constantly pressured Tom for more than he wanted to give. She didn't want to join that crowd, not ever.

It was too nasty outside to work in the garden and too wet to cut the grass, so Janelle worked her way upstairs with a dust cloth, taking occasional swipes at the most obvious surfaces. She thought about going to Madison to spend the day with her sister-in-law, but felt too lazy. She was restless and bored, the kind of boredom that has no resolution, but stems from a vague discontent hard to pin down.

She'd all but decided on a visit to Madison when the phone rang. Racing down the stairs, she grabbed the receiver on the third ring.

"Hi, Janelle. It's Katherine. Were you upstairs or in the basement?"

"Upstairs. How're you doing? Is it raining down there, too?"

"Gorgeous sunshine here." Katherine's tone of voice changed perceptibly. "This isn't a social call, Janelle. I need your help."

"Me?" This was definitely a first.

"Yes, you. Tom Wineski's wife has filed a complaint that Tom violated part of his custody agreement when he took his daughter across the state line without her mother's permission. She's pressing the court to withdraw all his visitation rights."

"Oh, Katherine, that's awful. Can she do that?"

"She can try. The idea behind that clause was to keep Tom from taking Tippy when he went on location. Just another way of limiting contact and, initially, the family-court judge bought it. But this was a completely different situation—"

"It certainly was. She's the whole reason Tom had to bring Tippy to Jackson in the first place. What does the judge have to say to that?"

"He hasn't heard it yet. The hearing is set for Thursday afternoon. Would you be willing to come down and appear on Tom's behalf?"

"Of course I would. Do you think it will help?"

"I wouldn't ask you if I didn't think it would. So, I'll air out the guest room and set up the appearance. Can you come Wednesday night?"

"Actually, I can't, Katherine. I told Irene and Kathy I'd go with them to the planning committee meeting for Fall Fest. But I promise I'll be there before noon on Thursday. Should I meet you at the office?"

"I guess that'll be okay. I want to go over some of the questions the judge could ask and that sort of thing. And, Janelle, park your car at the condo and take a cab over. You'll absolutely never find a place to park near the office."

Janelle did her best to look like the typical Midwestern widow, dependable and honest. She wore her most conservative suit and left her hair up in the casual bun she wore most days. She was sure Katherine would have liked her to wear her usual housedress and apron, but that would have been pushing it.

The whole drive down Janelle worried about whether Tom really wanted her to come. Wouldn't he have called himself if it was his idea? Janelle was happy to help, no matter what the reason, yet she wished she was seeing Tom again because he wanted to be with her and not because she had something he needed.

His greeting was everything she could have wished for. When she arrived at Katherine's office he was already there, sitting on the couch in the waiting room, rubbing his forehead as if to erase a headache. He seemed lost in thought, maybe even worried. When he saw Janelle, the anxious expression vanished. He stood, smiling as she entered. "You look fantastic. It's great to see you again."

Those few words dispelled most of Janelle's fears. He sounded so sincere. She smiled at him, losing herself for a moment in the warmth of his eyes. "I look like I just got off the farm, which isn't too far from the truth, I guess. But it's great to see you again, too. And you *do* look fantastic." He was dressed in a dark suit with a subdued pinstripe. He was obviously trying for a sedate, composed image. He looked like a banker, but not like any she'd ever met. If this man had been a lending officer, the bank could have raised its interest rate two points and women would still have lined up for loans.

Katherine walked out of her office, startling both of them. "I hate to interrupt this mutual admiration society, but I need to brief Janelle." In a moment she was all business. "Come into my office, Nell."

Her briskness sobered both of them and Janelle followed Katherine. She sat opposite her sister and welcomed the return of the butterflies. It was a reminder of just how important today was to Tom.

She forced herself to remember how crucial this court hearing was, despite how wonderful it was to see Tom again.

She curbed her misplaced happiness and concentrated on what Katherine had to say.

Janelle's nervousness resurfaced again as she sat in the judge's waiting room several hours later. At least it had been an informal hearing in his chambers. Now as she waited, she reviewed her testimony and decided it hadn't been all that different from a talk with someone like her minister. Just a simple recounting of the conversation she'd overheard about why Tippy had come to Jackson. The judge had asked why Tom had spent the night at her house, and once again Janelle explained that he'd done so because Tippy had insisted. The whole thing had been short and painless with no questions from either attorney.

Elaine Wineski had been exactly what Janelle expected. She was almost as petite as her preteen daughter and had the same blondish hair. It was even styled similarly, worn long and all messed up. She wore a leather suit, much more sophisticated and expensive than the leather miniskirt Tippy had worn to Jackson, but the resemblance was striking. It occurred to Janelle that this was one woman who hated growing old and was fighting it every step of the way. If she felt that way, Janelle wondered why she wanted custody of a daughter who was bound to remind her of her age every day.

When the door opened and Tom's ex-wife stormed out, Janelle didn't even have to ask who'd won. Elaine gave Janelle a venomous look and left the office with her attorney at her heels. Katherine came out next, looking pleased but trying to hide it, and Tom brought up the rear, an elated grin confirming Janelle's conjecture. Janelle's smile mirrored his. At Katherine's nod, she followed them from the office.

They waited by the elevator in complete silence. It puzzled Janelle. She was excited even if the other two weren't. But she waited, a little afraid that maybe she'd been wrong and the hearing hadn't been decided in Tom's favor.

An empty elevator arrived and the three entered. As the elevator door slid shut, Tom shouted, "So much for decorum!" With a rebel yell, he grabbed Janelle in a bear hug that lifted her off the ground and rocked the elevator. "We did it! You did it! Katherine did it!" He set Janelle down gently and turned to give Katherine a hug. She held out a hand to stop him and pointed to the light. "First floor."

The doors slid open and the three exited, looking appropriately restrained. Anyone looking closely could see that Katherine was biting her lower lip to keep from laughing and Janelle's neatly pinned bun was now halfway down her back.

Janelle and Tom were seated in the waiting limousine before Janelle realized Katherine wasn't joining them. The limousine rolled away from the curb, and Tom reached for the bottle of champagne nestled in the ice bucket. Janelle watched the way he settled comfortably into the corner of the plush seat. It didn't come quite as naturally to her. She felt as though she were on stage, despite the fact that the windows were tinted and no one could see inside. The velour seats, the bar and the little TV were exactly as they should be. She was the one who was out of place.

"I haven't felt this fantastic since Tippy was born." As Tom handed Janelle a glass, their fingers entwined briefly as the glass changed hands. She could feel the excitement he was trying hard to contain. He turned to face her, angling his body in the corner of the seat.

She sipped the champagne and enjoyed the dry tingle of the bubbles. "You know, I've never been in a limousine before."

When he smiled at her she hoped he wasn't laughing at her naïveté. "How do you usually get around when you're in the city?"

"By bus and sometimes I bring my car." She settled back into the seat and took another sip of champagne. "This is an awfully comfortable way to travel."

He gave her his dynamite smile and moved closer. "Somehow I hear a 'but' lurking behind those words." He rested his hands on her shoulders and turned her so she faced the window, her back to him. "Come on, Nell, relax and enjoy it. I feel like celebrating." He squeezed her shoulders.

"Your hair is falling out of this bun thing. Let me take the pins out. You don't really want to wear it up, do you?"

It was a rhetorical question. He'd already tossed a handful of hairpins into the ashtray, and Janelle's nervousness found a new niche. Exactly how did he plan to celebrate?

She turned around in the seat and edged away from him, the sweet sensations radiating through her.

"So, Tom, what did the judge say? What happened after I left? Can you tell me?"

Tom took a deep breath and settled back in the seat. "Let's skip the details. Like the way Elaine made an absolute fool of herself or the fact that Katherine also had a statement from Mrs. Meltzer. The fact is, this whole episode can only help when Katherine files for a new custody hearing."

Janelle decided to risk the snub and ask the question that had occurred to her earlier. "Tom, I don't mean to invade your privacy or anything, but I don't understand why having custody of Tippy is so important to Elaine. I don't mean to sound unkind, but she just doesn't seem that motherly."

Tom didn't seem to mind the question. He took another sip of champagne, then put the glass down. "It's all a power play on her part. It started years ago. We separated before *Chicago's King* went into high gear. She thought the good times were over. Then King made it big and suddenly she wanted to reconcile."

Tom paused, as if editing his words, then shrugged his shoulders and plunged on. "I think I mentioned before that I'm not exactly proud of how I behaved in those days. I wouldn't even consider getting back together. Now, I know she loves Tippy in her own way, and I'm even willing to concede that she deserved custody then, but the fact is, she insisted on sole custody just to make me pay for my independence. At that point, I might have considered reconciliation for Tippy's sake, but like I said before, I never thought the judge would deny joint custody. My life is different now, but one thing that woman can do is hold a grudge."

"If she's so good at holding a grudge, what makes you think she'll let this incident end here?"

"Normally, I'd be worried, but I know for a fact that she's leaving for a cruise tomorrow because Tippy is coming to stay with me tonight. Elaine isn't going to be around to make any more trouble for at least a month. And I think Katherine plans to file sometime after Elaine gets back from this trip. Hopefully by then, I'll have had enough time with Tippy to make her see that I really care and want to have her with me."

"Surely Tippy knows that already."

"Listen, Janelle, Elaine has been doing a number on that kid for two years. I don't know exactly what she's been telling her, but Tippy doesn't think too much of me. Couldn't you tell this past weekend?"

"Well, sort of. I mean, she *did* seem to be a little argumentative. But all kids are like that at her age."

"No, Elaine is an expert at twisting the truth, and I've never had Tippy for any length of time to convince her otherwise. As a matter of fact, if it weren't for the creep Elaine is living with, I'm not sure Tippy would be willing to come stay with me now. She'd probably prefer Mrs. Meltzer."

The chauffeur spoke over the intercom, "First stop, Mr. Wineski."

The driver pulled into the circular driveway in front of Katherine's condominium. Janelle put her glass down and fought the wave of disappointment that the ride had seemed so short. She smiled at Tom, framing a charming goodbye speech that he interrupted before the third word. "Forget goodbye, Janelle. We have to celebrate. I won't be picking Tippy up until after her ballet class tonight, around nine-thirty. How about an early dinner?"

It had to be the champagne that made her feel euphoric. She bit her lip to control her smile. "I'd really like that, Tom."

His own grin broadened at her demure response. "Great, I'll send the car for you around six." He hopped out of the limo, waving the chauffeur aside and held the door for her.

"Just dress casually. We'll eat at my place."

Janelle wasn't sure that was a good idea at all. A nice public restaurant sounded a lot safer. In a crowd, his charisma would be diffused a little. Of course, in a crowd she wouldn't have a minute alone with him.

"Okay, Tom. How about if I bring dessert?"

Tom laughed out loud. "This isn't potluck, Janelle. Just bring yourself."

Right, she thought, and as few inhibitions as possible. She waved goodbye as the limousine eased into traffic. She headed for the apartment wondering what sort of casually elegant clothes Katherine had that she could borrow.

The steaks had thawed in the microwave, the potatoes were ready to bake and the salad was made. Tom opened the refrigerator and put the rum cake that had just been delivered inside. Gathering up the linen and silver flatware, he went down to the covered porch and set the table for two.

Whistling tunelessly, he experimented with a couple of arrangements and then set two places at right angles to each other. It looked more intimate that way, and intimacy was exactly what he was shooting for. He had one more chance to make a good impression on Janelle, and he wasn't going to blow it.

With a flick of the switch, he turned on the mechanism that converted the pool into a fountain. Walking along the side of the pool, he checked the candy-pink impatiens that lined its length. Janelle, that intrepid gardener, would be sure to notice any dead blossoms. He stopped at the other end and looked back toward the table. Perfect.

He checked his watch just as the doorbell chimed, then raced up the stairs, through the kitchen, and down the front hall—passing the formal dining room, living room and library before reaching the entrance hall and the door. He opened it just as she was about to ring again.

Despite the designer clothes, she looked like a teenager trying to sell ads in the yearbook, and just as nervous. The silky, off-white pants and matching silk sweater outlined her figure and her hair was loose and brushed away from her face, falling in casual disarray.

Oddly, the outfit emphasized her sweetness in a way the housedress and apron never had. These clothes were a hell of a lot sexier, too. Once he'd tried to picture Janelle all dressed up and had decided she wouldn't be the same. He'd been wrong. Janelle in sophisticated clothes was still the same Nell who liked rocking on the back porch on warm summer evenings.

By the time he'd escorted her back to the porch and left to get her a glass of wine, he could tell she was overwhelmed. For a minute he was annoyed. Why did they have to start from the beginning yet again? He'd hoped they were beyond that.

Was it being here that had her feeling out of place? Maybe it was the house. It was just a house—granted a big house—but just a place to live. He was on his own turf here. He should feel safer, more in control. Instead she made him feel almost as nervous as she was. What would it take to get her to relax? He was beginning to wonder if it was even worth the effort, worth the threat to his hard-won equilibrium. What did he want from her anyway?

Another kiss at the very least. He smiled at the thought. Another kiss like the one they'd shared on her back porch last weekend, then another and another. But even more than that, or at least as much, he wanted the friendship that Janelle had offered so unconsciously, the simple acceptance. There was plenty of room in his life for friendship, even intimate friendship.

For starters he wanted to feel the same ease with her now that he'd felt sitting in her kitchen. That was it! Tom snapped his fingers and laughed at his brilliance. He leaned out the door that led to the stairway down to the porch. "Hey, Janelle," he called. He waited until she came to the bottom of the steps. "Why don't you come up here for a few minutes. I could use a hand with the salad." He grabbed the bowl of greens he'd already prepared and stuffed it behind the milk and soda bottles on the middle shelf of the huge refrigerator.

"That's a wonderful room downstairs. It must be..." Her voice trailed off as she looked around the giant kitchen. Tom followed her eyes and watched her smile fade. Maybe if he kept right on talking, she would start to relax.

"Yup, that's my favorite room winter and summer. It's completely enclosed in the winter so I can swim laps down there or watch the snow fall. In the summer I can use the outdoor pool, so the gardener turns that one into a fountain."

"It must be cool even on hot days," Janelle said in what was little more than polite conversation.

When she didn't continue, he took her by the arm and kept right on talking. "Why don't you stand right here and cut up the salad stuff."

The pile of produce was neatly wrapped in cellophane and Janelle wrinkled her nose at it. "Do you suppose these store-bought tomatoes have any flavor at all?"

She gave Tom a look of reproof that reminded him of his third-grade teacher. "How can you buy this stuff after you've eaten the real thing?"

"This is the big city, sweetie. That's the way it comes here. How about if you supply me with the extra veggies from your garden. That would give you an excuse to come down every week." He was teasing, but the idea appealed to him.

He perched on the stool across the counter from her and peeled carrots while she washed the lettuce.

"Come to the city every week? Once a month is about all I can stand."

"What do you have against the city?" He paused in his chopping, more interested in her answer than he would have cared to admit.

"It's so impersonal." Her answer was prompt. She'd obviously given this some thought. "I can't stand the way people don't even see you. No thank-you's, no courtesy at all. I mean, sometimes it seems that snarling is the standard way of communicating."

She chopped celery into bite-size portions and shook her head.

"Oh, come on, Nell, it's not all that bad. People are always polite to me."

She gave him a look that wasn't difficult to interpret. "Tom, I think we've already established that our lives are significantly different. You're mansions and limousines. Me, I'm farmhouses and public transportation. Obviously, our perspectives are going to be just a little different."

"Vive la différence!" He made her laugh and decided to pursue the subject a little further. "Is that why you left the city when your husband died?"

"There were a lot of reasons, but that wasn't one. I'd lived in cities all my life, they were all I knew. Arnie and I never considered small-town life. It was the economics of being a widow that was one of the major reasons Dan and I moved to Jackson. I knew I could probably make ends meet in a small town. When you get away from the city, the cost of living declines dramatically. I mean, Arnie had some good insurance policies through work, but it's really expensive raising a child these days. And I knew that I wanted to be available for Dan when he was that young." Janelle stopped talking abruptly. "Sorry, I didn't mean to go on so."

Tom smiled away her embarrassment. "Nothing to apologize for. You're right, though. Our life-styles *are* different. I thought you did all that gardening and baking because you liked it.''

"Oh, I do. But there's no denying that it helps stretch the money when you grow your own food and put up whatever's extra.''

She shrugged and looked around the room once again, and Tom paused to follow her eyes. He could tell she felt more comfortable now. "This house is incredible, Tom. It looks like one of those mansions they use in the nighttime soaps.''

He nodded, his thoughts distracted. Forget the house. He wanted to know more, like the rest of her reasons for leaving the city and whether she would ever consider moving back. On the other hand, that sort of question seemed a bit premature.

"Yeah, I know what you mean. My agent bought it for me when I first came here—to keep up the image, I guess.''

"It does that.''

The fact was, the house suited his life-style just fine. He'd worked long and hard to project his image. He stood up and rummaged through the cupboards for the salad-dressing ingredients.

"Actually, this kitchen is great.'' She shook her head in disbelief. "Two sinks. Hardly essential, but I guess an extra one could come in handy.''

She'd completed her inspection and turned back to face him. "I'm impressed that you seem to know where everything is.''

"Hey, I spent all afternoon learning.''

Janelle laughed again, and the tone for their evening was set.

By the time they finished dinner, they'd laughed so hard and so long that Tom suggested they perfect an act as stand-up comedians. The stuff of his childhood had never seemed quite so amusing before, but somehow Janelle made even the rough spots seem funny.

They sat side by side on the love seat that was part of the porch's year-round furnishings. It was still light, though darkness was settling fast, and the sound of the fountain barely masked the suburban night sounds outside.

Janelle curled up on the seat beside him. Her feet were bare, her shoes having been abandoned long ago. She faced him, her eyes animated and smiling. "My theory, not that it's terribly profound, is that everything you've done makes you what you are now." She paused looking a little puzzled. "I guess that's a pretty obvious theory. Maybe it isn't mine after all." She giggled.

"Janelle, just how much wine do you usually drink?" He eyed her suspiciously, trying to remember how many times he'd refilled her glass.

She held up her hand. "Tom, I am not the *slightest* bit drunk. I'm very relaxed, but that's because you're so much fun to be with, and we've laughed ourselves punchy over the last hour or so." She shifted as though she was going to stand up and Tom stopped her. He knew she could read his mind. She settled back on the love seat. As she turned to face him, he watched those incredible eyes, the hazel fading away to blue. "Oh, Tom," she said with a sigh, "I think we've told enough jokes, don't you?"

His lips were a fraction away from hers. "Janelle, I've never been more serious in my life."

He remembered the other times he'd held her, the other time he'd kissed her and thought he knew what to expect. But before she'd been more observer than participant. This time she wanted the kiss as much as he did. He was gentle, she was demanding. His slow, tender kiss changed rapidly as she slid her hands under his loose cotton jacket. Despite his shirt, he could feel the warmth of her hands as they caressed his back, pulling him closer to the slow sensuous movement of her body.

The silken fabric of her slacks heightened his arousal, and he slid his hand along the satiny fibers and imagined her skin under his fingers. She would be just as soft, but warm to the touch, then even warmer with wanting. As he urged her body to more intimate contact with his, Janelle's lips parted, deepening the kiss, wanting more.

He ached to kiss all of her, but let his hands communicate instead, moving up past her waist, under her sweater to her full breasts, hardening beneath his touch. She moaned a little as he withdrew his tongue and traced her mouth. Her lips took control now, and he let her explore his face and mouth. He could feel the desire building, as her lips branded his skin.

A single chime sounded and a marked silence descended. Janelle stiffened immediately. Tom recognized it as the automatic shutdown on the fountain's timer.

He held Janelle close a minute more, released a long breath and spoke, his voice tinged with regret. "I have to pick up Tippy."

Janelle nodded. She struggled to sit up, straightened her clothes and started to search for her shoes. Tom felt a little embarrassed himself. Here he'd just spent the better part of five days convincing a judge he could be "Father of the Year," and he'd almost forgotten to pick his daughter up because he had a hot date. Time to stop thinking like a lover.

He shook his head and stood up from the love seat, trying to shake off the sensual longing that lingered. Think like a father, he commanded himself.

Janelle was waiting in the kitchen by the time he caught up with her. "Janelle, honey, listen, I'm sorry. We didn't even get to the dessert."

Her impish smile took the bitterness out of her words. "Oh, I don't know, Tom, I kind of liked the dessert we chose, didn't you?"

He smiled back, grabbed her hand and kissed the back of it in one fluid motion. "It was fabulous," he growled. "Come on, I'll drive you back to Katherine's. It's on the way."

The old Porsche sat waiting in the driveway. Janelle still thought it a hideous heap of graying, rusting metal, but right now it gave her an excuse to sit close to Tom, and for that she would tolerate a dune buggy.

They turned out of the driveway and were cruising toward the expressway before either of them spoke.

"Janelle, I want to ask you something pretty important."

He sounded serious and Janelle gave him her full attention. "Sure, Tom." She could think of a lot of things he might ask, and she wouldn't say no to any of them.

"I couldn't be happier about having Tippy for the month, you know that." He looked at her as he braked for a red light.

She nodded. The light changed and he pulled away from the traffic. The car might not look like much, but its engine was certainly in fine tune.

"But I *do* have one problem. I have to go down to Mexico at the end of next week to shoot a cameo appearance in a movie. Normally I'd think about taking Tippy with me, but I know this crew, and it really isn't an appropriate atmosphere for a young girl. Do you think she could spend the week with you in Jackson?"

Janelle felt as though she'd reached the top of the roller coaster and was now plummeting downward. That's what this was all about. The intimate little dinner, the tantalizing kiss, all so he could get a baby-sitter for his daughter. How far would he have been willing to go to assure her cooperation?

She was silent so long that Tom eased up on the accelerator and looked over at her. "Janelle, if it's too much of a problem, I could work something else out."

Good manners and her "help thy neighbor" mentality were too well ingrained in Janelle for her to even consider refusing. She spoke carefully, trying to ignore the lump in her throat. "Oh no, Tom, I'd love to have her come stay. Dan would enjoy it even more. You know everyone was counting on seeing you again." She hoped she sounded sincere and that her disappointment wasn't as evident as she felt it was.

Details were discussed, and by the time they reached Katherine's he was late. Their goodbye was rushed.

Tom stood by the door waving the doorman aside. "Janelle, thanks for everything. There aren't too many women I call 'friend,' and it really means a lot to me."

As she headed for the elevator, Janelle kept reminding herself of his words. She was different from the women in his little black book, and she told herself to be grateful for that. She was his friend.

Janelle had to laugh at the thought. The sexiest man in America and she was number one on his list of baby-sitters.

Six

___

Dating is totally stupid." The girlish voice drifted through the open back door, and Janelle couldn't resist eavesdropping. At the moment she was in total agreement.

"I've been on one date with this guy in high school and it was awful. I couldn't think of anything to talk about, and he wasn't interested in talking anyway."

Janelle paused while making the root-beer floats and tried to catch Dan's reply, but she couldn't make out his words.

"You got it," Tippy agreed, "but the phone calls I get from boys aren't nearly as bad as the dating stuff. I like it better here, the way everyone does stuff together."

It wasn't a subject meant for mothers' ears, and Janelle tried to tune out the voices. She'd done her best to let the kids have some independence, and the week had been pleasantly uneventful.

Except for some dandy scrapes from a fall off her skateboard, Tippy had suffered no ill effects from her enforced separation from her father. She didn't cry herself to sleep,

NO COST! NO OBLIGATION!
NO PURCHASE NECESSARY!

PLAY "LUCKY 7"
AND GET AS MANY AS SIX FREE GIFTS...

HOW TO PLAY:

1. With a coin, carefully scratch off the three silver boxes at the right. This makes you eligible to receive one or more free books, and possibly other gifts, depending on what is revealed beneath the scratch-off area.

2. You'll receive brand-new Silhouette Desire® novels, never before published. When you return this card, we'll send you the books and gifts you qualify for *absolutely free!*

3. And, a month later, we'll send you 6 additional novels to read and enjoy. If you decide to keep them, you'll pay only $2.24 per book, a savings of 26¢ per book. There are no hidden extras.

4. We'll also send you additional free gifts from time to time, as well as our newsletter.

5. You must be completely satisfied, or you may return a shipment of books and cancel at any time.

This may be your lucky play...
FREE BOOKS and FREE GIFTS???
Scratch off the three silver boxes
and mail us your card today!

PLAY "LUCKY 7"

Just scratch off the three silver boxes with a coin.
Then check below to see which gifts you get.

YES! I have scratched off the silver boxes. Please send me all the gifts for which I qualify. I understand I am under no obligation to purchase any books, as explained on the opposite page.

225 CIL JAYN

NAME

ADDRESS   APT

CITY   STATE   ZIP

7	7	7	WORTH FOUR FREE BOOKS, FREE SURPRISE GIFT AND MYSTERY BONUS
🍒	🍒	🍒	WORTH FOUR FREE BOOKS AND FREE SURPRISE GIFT
●	●	●	WORTH FOUR FREE BOOKS
🔔	🔔	🍒	WORTH TWO FREE BOOKS

she seemed less morose than on her first visit and, best of all, she actively participated in conversations.

Calls came daily from Mexico, but Tom spoke only briefly with Tippy. It wasn't just the bad connection that led to their stilted conversations. Tom was right when he said that the relationship needed work. In fact, Dan spent more time talking to Tom than Tippy did. Janelle deliberately kept her end of the conversations brief, though more than once Tom seemed inclined to chat.

In all honesty, Janelle had to admit that she was still miffed at the way she'd been manipulated. In the brief flare of passion they'd shared, Janelle had seen a future for the two of them. And that future hadn't included a week of baby-sitting Tom's daughter. Her disappointment had mellowed into pragmatic acceptance. Tom was used to getting what he wanted and would do what he thought necessary to get it.

His manipulation had hurt, though. For the first time in years, she'd been tempted to abandon her self-imposed isolation. The risks of an intimate relationship seemed worth it. Now his life-style, his values, seemed to preclude it. How could they ever get closer than friendship if that was all he wanted? It seemed he viewed anything more intimate as a way of getting what he wanted rather than as a way of expressing his feelings.

But how could she even be sure of *his* feelings when her own were so confused? She recalled the sleepless hours she spent trying to convince herself that the kiss they shared had been something more than a casual expression of affection that had careered out of control. Then she counted the other hours she'd spent convincing herself that Tom's friendship was more valuable and long-lasting than his attentions as a lover would be.

It was just that the feelings he'd aroused were difficult to forget. When she least expected it, memories of their kisses would filter through her mind and with them an undeniable rush of desire. If their friendship lasted long enough, maybe she could convince him that friends used a more direct approach and didn't play emotional volleyball.

Carefully balancing the tray, Janelle pushed open the screen door, and Tippy jumped up to hold it open for her. As expected, the conversation stopped once Janelle joined the duo, and the threesome sat in silence, watching the lightning that forewarned an approaching storm.

The chemistry of the Friday root-beer tradition had been altered in the last few weeks. The root beer still fizzed, the ice cream was just as sweet, but as the population on the back porch shifted from week to week, Janelle wondered if she and Dan had lost the camaraderie that had led to such good conversations in the past.

"Mom, you should see the awesome trick dive Tippy showed me. Can you come to the pool soon so I can show you?"

"Sure, Dan. I'll save some time tomorrow after your swim practice. How's the skateboarding coming? Have you gotten used to the knee pads yet."

"Sort of."

The qualified response caught Janelle's attention. "You know, when I was young, my mother wouldn't even let me play softball because she was afraid I'd get hit by the ball and lose my teeth or something." She waited to see if they were getting the message.

"I've been trying to convince Dan to use his more, Mrs. Harper. I mean, I'm not a sissy or anything, but I don't want to wreck my knees. He thinks it isn't macho to use the knee pads. Tippy rolled her eyes as she finished, making it perfectly clear how she felt about that.

"Okay, okay." Dan's words bore the ring of long-suffering. "You two don't have to nag. I hear you."

The phone rang and Dan jumped to answer it.

The thunder rolled in behind the lightning now, but judging from the time lapse between flash and boom, the storm was still a good way off.

"Do you think we should go inside, Mrs. Harper? My mother always makes me come in at the first sign of rain."

It sounded as though Tippy subscribed to the same school of thought. Janelle glanced her way. The child was sitting on the edge of her seat.

"Would you feel better inside? The storm really is a good distance away yet. I like the way the air cools, and you can almost feel the electricity."

"I don't mind staying out as long as you think it's safe." Janelle smiled and nodded her understanding as Tippy settled back into the chair and pulled her feet up on the edge, staring off into the night. She was touched by the child's trust in her. More than that, she felt an irrational swell of happiness that Tom's faith in her as a guardian for his daughter hadn't been misplaced.

"You know, except for the rain thing, my Mom lets me do almost anything I want. It's my Dad who always comes down on me. I don't know why he hates me so much."

It would have been easy to disclaim the latter, knowing how much Tom cared for Tippy. Janelle just kept rocking. "Like, what sort of things does he do?"

Without hesitation Tippy began her litany. "Oh, he makes me go to bed by ten. He won't drive me to school, I have to take the bus. He makes me do my homework before I can watch TV. And even this week, he wouldn't let me stay by myself while he was away."

Janelle wasn't about to admit that it sounded like pretty responsible parenting to her. She tried to look at it from Tippy's point of view. "And your Mom has different standards?"

"Real different. She isn't always checking up on me. She says living with Dad would be awful because he's just trying to impress people by having me around. I wish he'd get over that part and just ignore me." The cynicism was there, but underlying it, a fear that her mother was telling the truth.

"You know, Tippy, when my parents divorced—"

"Your parents were divorced?" Tippy's surprise was genuine. "I didn't know anybody got divorced back then."

It sounded like she meant "back in the stone ages."

"It wasn't real common, but it happened even then." Janelle paused. If Tippy didn't want to hear about it, she wouldn't push.

"So..." The child watched Janelle intently.

"Well, it took me years before I realized that even though my parents hated each other, they loved me. They would say bad things about each other all the time, and I was at least fifteen before I realized that what they were saying just wasn't true."

"But how did you know that they weren't true? How did you know that your Dad really loved you?" The cynicism was gone, and there was such anguish in her voice that Janelle prayed her words would help.

"I knew because he told me he did, and he never did anything to prove otherwise. He made me do things I didn't want to do, like making my bed and finishing my homework, but he never ignored me and he was always glad to have me around. Despite what my mother said, I began to realize that what she was really afraid of was that I'd love Daddy more than her and she would be all alone."

"Yeah, I know how she feels. I hate being alone, too."

The topic was closed. Janelle would have liked to talk more about being alone and being lonely. Heaven knows she'd had enough experience of that in the last five years. Add the aching loneliness she'd felt this week and she could speak as an expert. But it would have to wait for another Friday night.

Lightning and thunder startled both of them, and they immediately jumped to their feet.

"I don't know about you, Janelle, but I'm going in."

"I'm right behind you, Tippy. That was close enough even for me."

"That was awesome, Dan! You'd get a ten for that dive. Wasn't it great, Janelle?"

Tom watched from the parking lot as Tippy gave Dan a thumbs-up and then mounted the steps for her dive.

"Now watch the footwork on this one, it's the secret to getting the extra height." Adjusting her suit straps and shaking her hands at her sides, Tippy concentrated on the dive.

Tom had seen Tippy dive more times than he could count. On the other hand, he'd never seen Janelle in a bathing suit, so he focused on her.

She looked wonderful. He'd seen dozens of better bodies littering the beaches of Acapulco, but none of them were more appealing to him than Janelle Harper, poolside in Jackson, Wisconsin. Maybe it was because he knew exactly how perfectly her body fit with his, the way his hands spanned that perfect waist and how her breasts filled his palms. Maybe it was because he liked the mystery of pinned-up hair and the innocent vanity of those painted toenails.

You're brilliant, Wineski, he congratulated himself. Having Tippy spend the week with the Harpers was a great way to guarantee that you'd see Janelle again.

He watched as Janelle applauded Tippy's dive and then resisted their urgings for her to try. He opened the car door, ready to walk over to the fence and add his two cents when he reconsidered. As much as he would like to tease Janelle onto the diving board, it probably wasn't a wise idea to call attention to himself. The car he was driving fit right in with the rest of the cars in the parking lot. Why bother renting something to blend in if he was going to announce his presence in so public a place?

The whistle blew and a lifeguard yelled, "Kids' break, ten minutes." Most everyone clambered out of the pool. As Tippy and Dan made their way to the snack bar, Tom watched as Janelle slipped into the water. There were a dozen or so other adults who took advantage of the break to swim laps, and he watched Janelle as she moved from one end of the pool to the other. It would be fun to be in the pool with her, preferably someplace more private, like his own backyard. They wouldn't need swimsuits and they wouldn't need to swim laps to burn off energy. He watched her long slim legs as they kicked a steady beat and imagined them moving to a more intimate rhythm.

He started up the car and flicked on the air conditioning. He would go back to Janelle's and wait on the back porch. It couldn't be any hotter there than it was sitting in this parking lot.

The streets were empty, and Tom swung an extra block out of his way and drove down Main Street, reminding himself of his first trip and his disparaging thoughts. It certainly looked different now. Where once it seemed shabby and almost ugly, now it was comfortable and unpretentious. The 25 mile-per-hour speed limit seemed plenty fast enough. After all, if it only took a few minutes to get where you were going, who needed to go fast?

All during the shoot, the days and nights of heat, frayed tempers and hectic partying, he kept reminding himself that in ten days he would be back in Jackson. When the heat grew unbearable, he imagined Janelle's garden and the shade of the fruit trees. When the local police suggested they not walk alone after dark, he remembered sitting on the street corner with Janelle waiting for Tippy's bus. When the leading lady offered him her body, he remembered Janelle and the kisses they'd shared. They may not have made love yet, but he knew her better and more intimately than most of the women he'd slept with. Thank God those charades were a thing of the past.

Janelle's back porch was almost as cool as he imagined and he sat in the shadows, his feet up on the railing, waiting. He was looking forward to the weekend, but had yet to make any concrete plans. First he would have to spend some time with Tippy. As much as he wanted to focus his attention on Janelle, his daughter had to be his first priority. It was ironic that after all these years, with Tippy as the sole focus of his efforts, his interest could be torn so. Over the past week he'd even worried about whether a relationship with Janelle would endanger his custody suit. He'd decided not. Janelle was as wholesome a companion as any judge could want. Besides, she was rapidly becoming an essential part of his life.

A gust of wind spiraled through the air and Tom closed his eyes, listening as it whispered through the yard. The trees rustled, the weather vane on the garage creaked and the smell of the garden blew his way. In that moment Janelle's back porch was close to heaven on earth. Almost. He needed Janelle beside him before he could call it perfection.

"You know, Janelle, I think I could live here forever." Tippy skipped along beside Janelle as Dan followed about forty yards behind. As usual, he'd forgotten his thongs and was walking slowly to avoid all the stones in the road.

Janelle smiled at her. "Why do you say that?" She could hardly believe that this was the same girl who'd come to stay a week ago. She was even farther removed from the insolent, near-adult who'd arrived in a miniskirt and green hair.

The twosome turned the corner at Whitewater and headed down the sidewalk toward the back door. "I like it here because there's so much to do, and all your friends are close enough so you can just ride your bike to visit them. I don't know, it's just neat . . ."

Tippy turned as Dan called out to her and hurried back down the sidewalk toward him. She called back to Janelle, "I just wish I didn't have to go back to Chicago."

"Is that my cue to ask if we can both stay for the weekend?"

Janelle recognized the voice and hurried down the walk to the back steps.

"Tom!" Her delighted surprise was genuine. For just a second she regretted her appearance. Her hair was drying into an uncontrollable mop. Of course she didn't have makeup on, but then friends didn't preen for each other, right?

As she reached the top step, he engulfed her in a hug that included her beach bag and towel. It felt so good to be in his arms again, even if it was just a friendly gesture on his part.

His fierce hug reminded her of more than friendship, and she felt a knot of desire twist through her. She let the sensation overwhelm her for a moment, then pushed out of his arms and gave him her most amiable smile.

"We didn't expect you until late tonight." He smiled at her and she chattered on. "Mexico obviously agreed with you. Hours of work and a long plane ride and you look better than ever." She was aiming for friendly, but even *she* could hear the yearning in her voice. She dashed to the porch railing and called, "Hey, hurry up, Tom's here!"

In the flurry of handshakes and hugs, it became clear that Tom was indeed staying for the weekend. "I've already dropped my stuff off at Kathy and Ned's."

Janelle felt a stab of disappointment and then acknowledged to herself that it would have been an exquisite torture to have him staying in her home and not in her bed.

The foursome crowded into the kitchen and made sandwiches, but lunch was an afterthought. The kids spent the entire half hour giving Tom every detail of the week. Janelle sat back and tried to come to terms with her conflicting emotions. With him sitting beside her generating an undeniable electricity, she wasn't sure she could be satisfied with a casual friendship. Common sense whispered friends, but the reality of his magnetism shouted more.

"How about it, Janelle?" Tom's direct question brought her back to the topic at hand. When she looked puzzled, Tom repeated his suggestion. "I thought maybe the kids and I could do something together and give you a break. I bet they've been running you ragged."

Within five minutes the kids had coerced Tom into going to check out the Mustang with them. The long-standing "Mustang issue" was the most convenient vent for Janelle's mix of confusion and frustration. "Dan, I don't know why you insist on acting as though you're buying that thing. I've told you a hundred times, it's out of the question."

Her three lunch companions looked surprised at her outburst, but it was Tom who played peacemaker. "We're just looking, Janelle." He turned his attention to the kids. "After that, Janelle's going to show me the sights. Do you guys think you'll be all right alone for a little while?"

"Show you the sights in Jackson? Really, Tom, besides the new firehouse and library, there isn't a thing to see." She sounded like a petulant child and tried to soften her words with a smile. It was only an imitation of the real thing and for a minute she thought she would burst into tears. Why in the world was she behaving like this?

"I've got too much to do," Janelle lied, then remembered it was the truth. "We're going to an ice-cream social at church tonight. The kids have been talking about it all week. They're going to rope off an area for the kids twelve and over and have a band. I said I'd take them and be a chaperon." It sounded perfectly hideous to Janelle. A night spent swatting mosquitos and listening to DC and his band try to sound like Duran Duran. Maybe Tom would opt for something else.

"If that's the plan, count me in, too. I'll bring the bug spray if you bring the earplugs. Now do you think I could see a smile? I've been living on dreams for a week."

The smile came because his words mirrored her thoughts, not because they were so beguiling and his eyes so compelling. Why did he have to be so patient and charming, when she was just itching for a fight? The smile faded, she broke eye contact and stood up from the table. Lunch was over.

When Tom left with the kids, Janelle headed for the garden, desperate for its soothing magic. As she weeded and culled the fading plants, she sorted through her own emotions.

By the time the last tomato was picked Janelle's equanimity was restored. She was Tom's friend, something in short supply in his life. And friendship had its advantages. There wasn't the vulnerability that came with a more intimate relationship, and there was still the chance she could come through this with her heart whole.

* * *

The ice-cream social was an annual event and well attended. At first Tom's star status threatened chaos, but Tom insisted he was going to be a regular fixture in Jackson and no longer qualified as a celebrity. That focused attention on Janelle, who wondered, with the rest of the crowd, exactly what was attracting him to the small town.

The streetlights had flickered on by the time the foursome headed home.

Janelle and Tom walked behind the two children, who were laughing and joking, punchy from fatigue and fighting the thought that the day was coming to an end.

Tom slowed, pulling Janelle into a bone-crushing squeeze. "I can't thank you enough for taking Tippy this week. She's like a different person, acting twelve instead of twenty. I bet she hasn't cried once."

"She's been great. But then I imagine Jackson has a lot to do with that. I really can't imagine Dan growing up anywhere else." Right now, walking arm-in-arm with Tom, Jackson seemed like heaven on earth.

"You told me once that there were a lot of reasons you decided to move here. I guess Dan was one of the biggest, right?"

He kept his arm around her shoulder, and Janelle moved a little closer. "It was really for Dan most of all. I wasn't sure how I'd adjust, being so used to living in the city. I didn't know what it would be like living so close to my in-laws either. But I thought Dan needed some male role models and Arnie had three brothers here, as well as his parents. I thought Dan could be a part of their lives and not lose touch with his father."

"And you were willing to sacrifice your own happiness for that?"

He made it sound like she was a candidate for sainthood. "It was really important to me. At the time I never thought I'd ever be happy again anyway. Besides, I promised myself when Dan was born that I'd always put his needs before my own; that he was more important to me than anything else."

Tom prompted her. "But you got over your loss and came to like living here."

"That about sums it up. Living here grew to be really special, mostly because of the pace of life and the people, of course. I know what they expect of me and I know what I can expect of them. It's different in the city. You can't know everyone and, God knows, you never know what to expect from one minute to the next."

"I'm glad Tippy's had the chance to experience it. I have you to thank for that."

Janelle closed her eyes and took a deep breath. "I would have done the same for any friend, Tom. She's been a pleasure to have around."

His conversation was so pleasant, so friendly, so lacking in passion that Janelle wanted to kick him in the shins. Instead, she sorted through her dozen definitions of friendship and picked the one that started with "platonic."

With that in mind, Janelle slipped out of Tom's arm on the pretext of picking up a piece of newspaper littering the sidewalk. She tossed it in a nearby bin. Tom didn't take the hint. He caught up with her and put his arm around her once again.

"Janelle," Tom whispered, his lips brushing lightly on the sensitive pulse point behind her ear.

"Platonic" faded from her vocabulary as she tried to control the urge to turn her mouth to his lips.

"I want to spend the day with you tomorrow."

Janelle looked down at her feet, avoiding his eyes. Maybe he meant a family sort of outing. She whipped through her list of definitions and opted for "social." Caution edged her voice. "That sounds nice. We could take Tippy and Dan—"

"No, Janelle. I said 'you,' and I meant that singular, as in you and me, alone, together." They'd stopped walking, pausing in the middle of the deserted sidewalk.

"Oh, I don't know, Tom." What she really wanted to say was that it would be heaven. She faced him now, her back against the brick wall of the bank. He wasn't standing all that close—actually he stood halfway cross the sidewalk, just watching her.

She wanted to ask all those questions about his intentions, but didn't want to sound Victorian. She was excited and a little afraid. It had been years since she'd been on a date that meant anything, with someone who meant something.

"I mean, what would we do?" Now that's a really stupid question, she thought. Tom smiled at her as if reading her mind, and she hurried into speech. "Really, I wasn't kidding when I said there's nothing to see in this town."

He leaned against the lamppost and crossed his arms. "We could try to catch fish at Lake Ripley. We could go on a picnic. We could even go to church together. I don't care, Janelle. As long as it's with you and without those two twelve-year-old chaperons."

Fishing might not be too bad. She would be distracted by the smell of the bait at least. Church was even better. "I guess we could go on a picnic."

Tom nodded agreement and moved closer until he had her in his arms. Low and full of secrets, his voice mesmerized her. "We'll find a nice quiet spot, maybe near the river or on the lake. There'll be big beautiful trees, no ants, no rocks, just a carpet of soft, cool grass. Can you picture it?" She nodded, caught up in the imagery, willing him to continue. "You can spread the blanket and I'll carry the basket. We'll watch the fishermen and eat our lunch. Then we'll stretch out on the blanket and . . ."

He kissed her gently. She could taste his longing in the intimate touch until her restraint broke and she pressed her mouth against his with an urgency borne from days of denial. Tom welcomed the demand, and responded in kind. Using his hands to turn her head slightly, he held her mouth with his, keeping her a willing prisoner of their rising passion. He teased her lips with his tongue, invading her mouth in an intimate imitation of the images in her mind. Lost in a kaleidoscope of feeling, Janelle revelled in the sensual fire that spread through her, pressing him closer. She didn't want the kiss to end. She wanted it to go on and on, over the edge of awareness to a world that was theirs alone.

"Oh, Janelle," Tom whispered against her neck. His words were a sigh of longing, of promise. The two stood, staring at each other, willing the hours to pass.

Before Janelle was quite steady on her feet, Tom urged her away from the wall and when she stumbled he pulled her into the shelter of his arm. In that moment, the facade of friendship disappeared. Now they were more than friends, still less than lovers, and happy.

Seven

More than a friend, less than a lover. How long would this midway point in their relationship last? Awakening from a night filled with erotic dreams, Janelle wondered where her restraint had gone. She could hear sounds from the kitchen. Probably Tippy and Dan getting ready for the swim meet. It was early yet. Without looking at the clock, she snuggled back under the covers, groaning at the soreness in her shoulders. She pulled the sheet up with an empty wish for more sleep. The sensual dreams had faded, but the tumult of emotion remained.

In a few short weeks, Tom Wineski had wreaked havoc on her carefully structured world. His smile, his caring, even his alter ego King had seeped into the fiber of her carefully woven life, leaving it frayed and ready to rip at the seams.

Would she really consider an affair? Affairs didn't last forever, and someday Tom Wineski would walk out of her life. She recalled the loneliness she felt when Arnie had died, the sense of isolation from life that she welcomed at first and then grew to hate. Those feelings had faded. Surrounded by his family, Janelle found traces of her husband in their values, their interests, even the way they talked, and the reminders mellowed her loss.

When Tom Wineski called it quits, there wouldn't be any of him left behind. There would be no way to ease the pain of giving everything and losing it all. Why wasn't it possible to hold back just a little of herself so the pain wouldn't be so great?

After all, how could it be anything more than a short-lived fling? No matter how much Tom talked about coming to Jackson, as time went on his schedule would make it more and more difficult. His job was demanding. He wanted to be more involved in his daughter's life. She would demand more of his time than he realized. Face it, she argued, a fling is all she could have.

She treasured the role of friend. The caring and companionship they already shared were too precious to throw away. Why couldn't she be happy with that? She knew the answer. There was no way she could draw the line between friendship and the incredible desire that surged through her whenever they were together. She was already over the line. She was already more than half in love with him. All relationships were destined to grow and change. Maybe it would be best to surrender to her emotions and leave the rest to fate.

Janelle heard movement at the door and turned over, a muffled groan slipping out as she realized just how stiff she was.

Tom stood there and watched as Janelle squeezed her eyes together, then opened them again.

"Mornin', Nell. I thought you wanted to get going before noon, but you don't look quite ready to join the world. Maybe I should go and let you rest in peace."

Despite his offer, he made no move to leave. Her hair covered the pillow, a soft contrast to the crisp white cotton sheets. The top sheet rested on the swell of her breasts, a tantalizing inch more and he could see what he yearned to touch. It was taking every ounce of his self-control to stay in the doorway and not walk closer to check and see if she was as naked as she looked.

"No, don't leave." Her voice was soft with sleep and tinged with longing. "You could do me a big favor." Her smile was beckoning.

Not moving from his spot by the door, Tom leaned back and folded his arms. "And what does Sleeping Beauty have in mind?" He smiled. If it was anything less than a kiss, he was going to be mighty disappointed.

"Could you give me just a little back rub? My shoulders are stiff from all the work we put in last night at the social. I'd really appreciate it."

He abandoned his stance by the door and moved to the edge of the bed. He couldn't decide if this was better than a kiss or not. Either way, he decided, it was a good beginning. Sitting on the edge of the bed, he leaned over and pulled the sheet down a little as Janelle turned and settled on her stomach. It wasn't the ideal way to give a massage, at least not the kind he had in mind. But if he settled himself as intimately as he wanted, his legs straddling her back, she would know in an instant exactly how she was affecting him.

He used his left hand to brush aside the wisps of hair trailing down her neck and let his hand run down her back as though he were a pianist warming up by running his fingers over the keys.

He could feel her shiver in response and knew that her control was as fragile as his. He felt her stiffen before she spoke. "Wait, Tom, I don't know what I was thinking of—"

"Shh," he whispered, "this is perfectly innocent." Like showering together to save water, he added to himself. Some of her tension dissipated, and he began a slow rhythmic kneading of her shoulder muscles. He enjoyed the feel of her skin, soft and warm beneath his lightly callused fingers. A sprinkling of cinnamon freckles across her back made him realize how fair her skin was. He kept his movements gentle, using his thumbs to massage the tension out of the sweet spot at the base of her neck and across her shoulders.

He closed his eyes and focused his concentration on the feel of her as he massaged the tense muscles. As her body relaxed, little sounds of approval were his only critique and he could feel the muscles ease with each encouraging murmur. He moved his hands lower, concentrating on the middle of her back, working his hands around, barely brushing the sides of her breasts. He kept the pace steady and counted the freckles, debating which one to kiss first. He moved his hands lower still to the small of her back and leaned over to press his lips to her neck, letting his body cover hers.

Urgency fought with restraint. Tom held back, trying to control the tempo. Janelle's murmurs had stopped, but he could feel the response of her body, welcoming, wanting. He didn't allow his full weight to press onto her back, but used his arms to support himself on either side of her. He kissed a delightful little freckle behind her ear and she turned her head a little more, so he could kiss her cheek and the corner of her mouth.

He wanted to feel his skin against hers, but was trapped in the sexual pull of their embrace and unwilling to move. He contented himself with using his lips to feel and taste, memorizing the exact spots that seemed to elicit the most response.

He slipped to her side, lying closer still, on sheets that held the warmth of her body. His movement gave her the freedom to turn and face him.

"Tell me, Janelle," he whispered hoarsely, "do you have anything at all on?"

"No," she whispered back. The passion in her eyes was as much an invitation as her whispered reply, and Tom pulled the sheet down a fraction and took her mouth in a surging kiss while he gently rubbed her nipple, already peaked in response. He lowered his mouth to her breast, covering the lip, sucking and teasing with tongue and lips. The sighs were moans now as she ran her hands through his hair, her body twisting toward him with instinctive urgency.

Tom sensed the surrender and wanted nothing more than to give in to the elemental urge that drove them. But there was still a rational corner of his mind, an awareness that remained, in spite of his need. He knew, he'd known, when he walked into the room that she wasn't ready, at least not completely ready, to commit herself to him this way. God knows, he understood how the body could want before the mind and heart were ready. It didn't ease the frustration though, and for a minute he was selfish enough to consider seducing her. Momentary gratification and eternal regret, he decided. Easing the sheet over her, he lay beside her outside the covers, his head propped up on his hand.

Neither spoke for a moment. Janelle buried her face in the pillow, and Tom struggled to control the passion that had left him unaware of time and place.

"I'm sorry, Tom." Janelle's voice was muffled by the pillow.

"Shh," he whispered. He wanted to touch her hair, smooth it away from her face, but he knew even a single touch would shatter his tenuous self-control. "No apologies, Nell. But maybe we better hold off on the back rubs for a while, hmm?" He smiled as the tension faded.

She turned back toward him and laughed, a quiet, throaty sound that vibrated through Tom's whole body. He inched himself a little farther away.

"No doubt about it. How about if we blame it on subconscious suggestion? I really wasn't quite awake when I first saw you."

No coy disclaimer, no misplaced anger, only Janelle's honest response. How was it that this woman spoke to his heart? He let her good spirits give truth to his smile. "I know, let's blame it on Kathy. She was the one who suggested I come and wake you up."

The mention of Kathy's name was as effective as a cold shower. Janelle sat upright immediately, nearly knocking Tom on the floor in the process. "What! Kathy's here?

Good grief, what does she think is going on up here.'' She looked around for the clock. ''She wasn't supposed to come until ten.''

Tom stood up and began retucking his shirt and smoothing his hair. ''Nell, it's almost eleven. She told me about using your kitchen for canning today, and so I gave her a ride over with me. When she saw you weren't up, she sent me up to wake you and said she'd get our picnic ready.''

''Well, you can go tell her I'm definitely awake now and almost out of bed, no thanks to her.'' She shrugged her shoulders. ''And, thanks to you, my shoulders aren't the slightest bit sore anymore.'' A teasing smile and wave of her hand shooed him out of the room.

Tom left, feeling singularly dismissed. He headed back downstairs, concocting several stories that would pay Kathy back for her ill-conceived suggestion.

''I can't believe you told her I was snoring! I've never snored a night in my life.''

Tom opened the car door for her, then leaned in to give her a quick kiss. ''How would you know? By your own admission you've been sleeping alone for the last few years. I bet you snore so loud the neighbors hear you.''

''Keep it up, Wineski, and you may never find out.'' She grabbed the door and pulled it shut, forcing Tom to jump back from the curb. He swung open the back door, threw the cooler in and gave her ponytail a tug.

Janelle considered the weighty question of exactly where to sit, while Tom walked around to the other side of the car.

She wanted to inch over on the bench seat and sit close to him, but decided that using the seat belt would be more mature. Just because she felt like a teenager was no reason to act like one. Reminding herself she was over thirty and a responsible woman, she pulled the lap belt over and fastened it, as Tom slid into his seat.

She tried to pull her shorts down a little so they would cover her thighs. Why had she worn this stupid outfit? She might be feeling like a sixteen-year-old, but she certainly didn't have a teen's figure anymore. Her thighs were okay when she was standing up, but when she sat down they looked ghastly. In desperation, she covered her legs with the newspaper she'd brought along.

When she turned to face Tom, he wasn't the slightest bit interested in her thighs. He was watching her face. "Last night you said something about going to an auction. Is that still on?"

The way he was looking at her, she was more than willing to head to the nearest motel. His arm rested along the top of the seat, and he played with the end of her ponytail. Janelle knew there were no nerve endings in hair, but somehow her whole scalp tingled and the shivery sensation was delightfully distracting.

Too distracting. Her mind and emotions said she needed time. She wasn't about to allow her attraction to override common sense. She would stick with her original plan and cancel the motel, or at least put it on hold.

Clearing her throat to hide her smile, she pointed to the paper. "Sure is. It's out on Highway 26, only about fifteen minutes from here."

Tom pulled away from the curb after studying the map a moment.

"I don't know what to expect at this sale. It's run by some group from Chicago. No one ever has estate sales on Sunday in these parts." They chatted on about what they could expect to find, Tom asking about the going prices for the items he was familiar with. He found a way to make even the sedate Ford behave like a sports car, and their arrival a half hour before the scheduled opening gave them plenty of time to examine the various lots. Tom dropped Janelle off and went to park the car in one of the fallow cornfields along the road.

Janelle hurried into the house to get a quick look at the furniture, then made her way outside to the tables set up on sawhorses. Noting the lots she wanted, Janelle kept an eye out for Tom. The area was crowded with other bidders, but with his six-foot height, he should have stood out. She saw a couple of big men, but only one man who came close to Tom's size.

When he hadn't shown up by the time she registered, she was worried. Maybe he'd been mobbed by fans. She stood up and tried to spot an unusual crowd, but didn't see any. Standing by the sign-up desk, she continued to scan the group when someone tapped her on the shoulder.

"Pardon me, ma'am. Are you in line?" She only glanced at the man. His baseball cap was pulled low, and his cheek bulged with a plug of chewing tobacco. He wore a sloppy sport coat over disreputable jeans, like a dozen other junk men who swarmed around these farm sales. Only this man was younger and thinner.

"You idiot," she hissed, "I didn't even recognize you."

He slouched against the table, somehow conveying a pot belly and bow legs, neither of which he had.

"Even better than applause. I bet you thought the only role I could play was a punky Chicago cop."

She shook her head in amazement. "Where did you get that awful jacket?"

"Up in Kathy's attic. We spent a good hour this morning concocting this costume. Looks pretty good, huh?"

The auctioneer announced that it was ten minutes until the start of the sale, and Tom dragged Janelle back into the house one more time to see if there was anything he wanted to bid on.

"A ukulele? Tom, what would you do with that?"

"The same thing I do with my banjo, play it." They were alone in the basement while Tom rummaged through some old sheet music.

"I didn't know you played the banjo."

"You sure know how to keep my ego in line, Janelle. Do you mean to tell me you didn't see me on the Grammys last year, playing backup to that bluegrass group?" Despite the wounded tone, his eyes were full of laughter.

It was a good thing, because Janelle burst out laughing. "Oh, that must have been priceless."

Tom pretended indignation. Janelle started up the stairs, but Tom stood at the bottom with his hands on his hips. "Listen, Giggles, I was damn good. They gave me a standing ovation."

"Tom, I hate to tell you, but they gave your *body* a standing ovation."

"No way. Great bodies don't mean a thing to them, they're artists." He was teasing again. "Besides, how do you know? You've never heard me play. Just wait. I recorded it, and next time you're in Chicago, I'll play it for you."

A bell sounded, announcing the beginning of the auction, and Janelle and Tom hurried to find seats. It was tedious waiting through the calls on farm equipment and tools until they got to the household items Janelle wanted. Tom played his part to perfection, even to the bidding, and almost got struck with a rusting tractor that hadn't run in five years. He actually bought several power tools that he insisted were going very cheap.

Janelle shook her head, wondering if she had created a monster, then almost missed bidding on a 1950 hi-fi console that she got for a ridiculously low price.

"How will you get that home? It won't fit in the trunk."

She glanced at him, half watching the next item the auctioneer held up. "I have a deal with my nephew, Jason. He brings his truck out here and picks up whatever I buy and can't carry. I store it in my garage until the shop in Chicago wants to send a truck up for it."

He nodded and raised his paddle to start the bidding on a ghastly velvet painting. She grabbed his hand and held it. "Tom, that thing's awful." He raised his hand and hers, increasing the bid five dollars. "Hey, I'm playing the part. Don't you think a nude on black velvet is my style?" He leered at her and waggled his eyebrows as the auctioneer awarded him the lot. "We'll give it to Jason."

Janelle shook her head in exasperation. "Kathy would have your hide."

They left long before the auction was over, stopped by the cashier's desk to pay and loaded what they could into the car. The velvet painting barely fit into the trunk, but Janelle refused to leave it behind for her nephew.

While Tom stripped off his auction disguise, Janelle poured him a cup of coffee. They leaned against the car parked in the shade of a lone oak tree.

"How come you didn't bring the Porsche? Mind you, I'm glad you didn't because we couldn't have gotten half this stuff home."

"For one thing, I thought I'd attract less attention in something more conventional. But the main reason is that the water pump died and I didn't have time to fix it before I left for Mexico." He turned and smiled. "And when I got back, I was in too much of a hurry to get here to take the time to fiddle with it."

Janelle tried to ignore the way his smile made her want to move closer. "Uh, you do all your car work yourself?"

"Yeah. It's the way I relax. I forget all my problems that way, it's a great way to unwind."

It sounded awful to Janelle. The only thing she ever felt when she tried to fix a machine was frustrated.

"Right now I'm rebuilding the engine on an old VW for Tippy."

"Does it take that long? I mean, she won't be able to drive for four years, right?"

"No, it won't take four years even if I only work on it occasionally. Those old VWs have great engines. Simple and fun to work on. Why, the other day I took the carburetor apart..."

His boyish enthusiasm was so evident that Janelle gave every indication of complete attention. In spite of appropriate nods and responses, she let her mind drift, imagining a future that included a rebuilt car for her. A future that meant Tom came home to her every night and rarely got out to the garage to work on his current project. She knew it was a fantasy. And if it wasn't for the aching reality that fantasies never come true, it would have been perfectly harmless.

"...And I thought once I'm done, I'd drive it for her. You know, do her a favor and keep it in good condition until she's ready for it." Tom accepted Janelle's good-natured teasing without rancor, openly acknowledging he was motivated by self-interest.

Stowing the thermos back in the basket, Janelle got into the car carefully. The sun had heated the seat to sizzling, and she was smart enough not to let her bare legs come in contact with the hot plastic.

She reached over for the seat belt, and after struggling for a few seconds, gave the restraint an exasperated tug. She looked at Tom. "What's the matter with this stupid thing?"

He shrugged, and she twisted in the seat to get a better look. The belt was tied in a series of knots that could only have been man-made.

Biting her bottom lip to keep from laughing, she turned to Tom. "Gee, I wonder how that happened?"

He grinned back. "Gee, Janelle, I don't know. Maybe you better sit a little closer and use the middle seat belt, hmm?"

Shaking her head in mock exasperation, she slid closer. With his arm around her shoulder, they sped down Highway 26, headed for the ideal picnic spot.

The drive was fun, despite the fact that they passed nothing more than farm after farm and field after field of corn.

A short while later they pulled into the parking lot of the state park. It was a pretty setting along the river with trees and grassy areas. There were plenty of spots where they could have a little privacy. She said as much to Tom, adding, "That way, maybe you won't be recognized." She just wanted to be sure he understood exactly why she considered privacy important.

The afternoon was near perfect. A gentle breeze kept the bugs away and made the heat tolerable. The secluded riverside spot they found gave them a one-way view of a few fisherman, and they sat on the blanket watching two young boys fish with their father, counting the number of fish they lost.

Tom talked about his childhood in New Jersey. He'd never gone fishing with his dad, an insurance salesman, but they had gone to hundreds of sporting events together.

"I was in fifth grade when I realized that if I wanted, I could be the one on the field playing. Dad insists he never had that in mind, but once I decided that's what I wanted, both Mom and Dad did everything they could to make it happen."

High school had been the beginning of the pressure. "By my sophomore year, I knew that I had what it took to make it big. My folks and my high school coach spent weeks considering the best career moves."

While he talked about the sleepless nights before USC accepted him, Janelle listened, finding it hard to visualize a young and struggling Tom. When he talked about trying out for the pros and making choices between family and career, Janelle understood the pressures that had ruined his marriage.

"Elaine learned to rely on the money, to let it take my place until it became more important than I was."

By the time he found himself in television, he was beginning to believe that making money was all he was good for. As his contact with his daughter diminished, he'd almost convinced himself that all Tippy wanted of him was the material things he could give her. "But then Elaine took up with this Cliff jerk, and Tippy began to call more often. At first I thought she felt left out and lonely, then I realized she couldn't stand Cliff."

The idea of a new custody suit had grown out of those phone conversations, and for the first time since college Tom's self-image changed. He became something more than a money-making machine. He was a father, in practice, as well as in name. "Meeting you was the icing on the cake. You're the first person in years who sees me without the Hollywood glitter."

Janelle thought of herself as lots of things, but never as icing on the cake. "Oh, I don't know, Tom. I'm not any more immune to your charms than any other woman."

"Ahh, but at least you're charmed by the real me and not some publicist's idea of who I am. Don't you see—" He stopped himself. "No, I guess you don't. But believe me, Janelle. I'm more real with you than I am with anyone I can think of, even with Tippy. With her I try to project authority when I'm actually shaking in my boots."

They sat close to each other while Janelle played with a bunch of clover, fashioning the simple white flowers into a primitive coronet as they talked. With her crown in place, she made Tom a necklace, then handed it to him rather than putting it around his neck herself. She wanted to kiss him then, but sat back abruptly, feeling a bit like she was playing with fire.

The picnic basket was still open and Tom rummaged through, finding some fruit and another plastic bag of cookies. With the last of the coffee, they had a snack before collecting the crumbs and trash. The late afternoon shade wrapped them in a tranquil embrace. Even as the shadows lengthened, neither one of them felt inclined to leave.

Janelle stared up at the sky and the wispy white clouds that seemed like shreds of cotton stretched to their limit. "Is it perfect here or am I imagining it?"

She wasn't looking at Tom, but staring into the late afternoon sky, enjoying the sun on her face and the breeze in her hair.

"I can only think of one way to make it better." With a gentle tug on her ponytail, Tom brought her closer and took her in his arms. His lips touched hers as his arms cradled her against him. It wasn't a gentle first kiss, or a heartbreaking goodbye. It wasn't a kiss of unbridled passion. It was a kiss that made life perfect, that communicated a bond beyond camaraderie, that promised intimacy, that demanded a future.

Not content to let it end, Tom teased her mouth with his lips and tongue, pushing Janelle gently onto the blanket covering the grass. The smell of the clover necklace crushed between them blended with the sounds of nature around them. It took very little imagination to transport them to a primitive paradise where only the two of them existed.

Tom brushed her hair from her face and kissed each temple. Kissing her once again, his mouth welcomed her touch as her tongue met his in an arousing duel. Then he began a slow erotic massage that ended with her breasts captured in his hands. As she arched in response to his caress, Janelle slipped her hands from his neck down his arms, until she clung to him, her legs parting to accommodate his arousal.

Janelle pressed her lips to his neck, feeling the strong pulse that conveyed the urgency she herself felt. His lips tickled her ear. "Oh, Tom." Janelle breathed the words against him and tried to regain some self-control.

Tom rolled on his side, his body still close to her. "You know, if we both weren't fully dressed—"

"I know, I know," Janelle interrupted. The thought was dangerous enough without voicing the words. They lay for a moment staring at each other. Janelle watched the edge of arousal fade from Tom's eyes, but the passion lingered. She turned her eyes to the dusky sky and thought of his eyes, their color mirrored in the deepening blue. How could she want something so badly and still be unsure of her place in his life? More than a friend, less than a lover had been fine for last night. Today it was inadequate. She sighed. "I guess we should go home. When were the kids expecting us?"

She didn't wait for an answer, but sat up and began gathering their belongings. The dusk was becoming night and the air was cooling rapidly. As her own passion was tempered, she tried to think reasonably, but her thoughts were jumbled by a profusion of feelings that left her shivering, partly from the cold and partly from her confused emotions. She ached for the closeness she and Tom could share. And she wanted more than physical closeness, though at the moment it was impossible to deny the sexual longing that clouded her thoughts. Did Tom really want the closeness, the commitment of an intimate relationship? How could she ask him to make time for her when everyone else wanted a part of him, too?

She closed her eyes with a surge of tear-filled self-pity. Would it ever be possible? Would something, someone, someplace always interfere? When was it her turn? When was she the one who came first?

"The kids probably haven't even missed us," Tom mumbled as he pushed himself into a sitting position. "But, you're right. It's time to head back." Janelle was too far ahead of him to hear.

He watched as Janelle hurried away. Her confusion was obvious. Why was she running away from something so obviously wonderful? Brushing the grass and dirt from his legs, he folded the blanket and followed her down the trail, trying to decide whether to confront her now or wait. Wait for what, he asked himself. Wait until there are a dozen people around? Or wait until he was back in Chicago and had to rely on the phone? It was now or never.

In five minutes they were back by the car, alone in the parking lot. The silence was strained, the tension tenable. Opening the back door, Janelle put the cooler on the floor. He watched her from a distance, then hurried to catch up with her. Seizing the opportunity, he used his arms to trap her between the car and his body. He tried to concentrate on the metal frame digging into the palms of his hands and ignore the already familiar feel of her body pressed against him.

"Janelle, listen, I want to resolve one thing before we head home."

She met his eyes. "It's all right, Tom. I understand."

"Nell, you don't understand, damn it. If you did, you wouldn't look like you were on your way to an execution." He held her chin with his hand and moved the rest of his body so she had a little breathing room.

"What we shared today meant a lot to me. Every part of today—the auction, the driving, the talking and the kissing. All of it meant that we have something. A future, Janelle. I think we have a future, don't you?" He didn't like the pleading note he heard in his voice and wondered why his usual arrogance had deserted him.

He watched as her tension lessened. He felt a surge of relief and then watched her eyes fill with tears. She didn't smile.

"I don't know, Tom, I just don't know." She lowered her head, but Tom could still see the tears. "And I'm afraid to take the chance to find out."

He let go of her chin and gathered her close, trying to understand how she could possibly have any doubts. "That's what life is all about, taking chances. You've taken them before, and they've paid off. What's stopping you now?" He felt more protective than loverlike right now and angry at himself for causing her pain.

Janelle pushed out of his arms. Obviously she wasn't feeling as vulnerable as he thought. She looked at him. "I don't know where I stand with you—if it means as much to you as it does to me. I mean, when I first got to know you, I thought you just wanted a friend, another single parent to share things with." She stared up at him, watching him intently.

"That's part of what I want," he said, answering carefully.

"Even when I came to Chicago for the custody hearing, I was still thinking friendship, but after that dinner I began to think about more than friendship. But then I wasn't sure how you felt."

"God, Janelle, how could you have any doubts? That was a pretty hot scene."

She turned her face away from him. Was she embarrassed? "Tell me the truth, Janelle," he insisted.

"It wasn't like you asked me to come down for purely social reasons, and then you asked me to baby-sit for Tippy right after, you know, right after that dessert we never got to." She smiled at the memory. "I thought maybe the kisses were a way of getting me to go along with—"

"*Janelle.*" The word conveyed only a part of the disappointment he felt.

She held up her hand as if to brush aside his dismay. "Really, I had a good look at exactly how manipulative you can be when I first met you. That whole first weekend I was never sure when you were on or off." She stood, still trapped between him and the car, her arms crossed defensively. "You said to be honest."

"So I did. Listen, Janelle, I thought we'd gotten way beyond that sort of game playing. After that first kiss on your back porch, I've never been anything but honest with you. I told you, Janelle, you're closer to the real me than anyone I know. That means a hell of a lot to me. As a matter of fact, it's damn scary to feel this vulnerable. I hope that means something to you. It does, doesn't it?"

She relaxed a little, obviously thinking back on the truth of his words. "Yes." She sounded surprised, then cautious. "It's too much like a dream come true, though." She sighed. "But, Tom, I'm still not sure exactly how much of a future we have. I mean, there's so little time for us."

He hugged her hard and stepped away. "Listen, sweetheart, I don't mind resolving past problems, but let's not look for some where there aren't any, okay?"

"You're the one who brought up the future. Don't you think we should be realistic?" He smiled at the tentative way she asked her question. She was looking for reassurance. That he could handle.

"Hell, no." He pulled her close, his lips crushing hers in a single blazing statement of intent. "I've spent my life beating the odds. I'm not going to stop now."

Eight

Daddy, I wish you could help me with my math. I just don't understand multiplying negatives.'' Papers were strewn all over the dining room table, but Tom's attention was focused on the telephone and the conversation with his daughter.

"I wish I could help too, honey. But it would be pretty tough to handle over the phone. Why don't you see if your mom will let you come over tomorrow night, and we can work on it then?"

Tippy made the arrangements with Elaine and ended the phone call. Tom turned back to the script on the table, pretending to look through tomorrow's scenes.

In fact, other scenes were running through his mind. The last three weeks hadn't played out anything like he thought they would. He has happy with the way his relationship with Tippy was developing. Her smiles meant more to him than all the points in the Arbitron ratings. But Janelle had been right when she said it would take time. It seemed he was forever sacrificing his own wants to accommodate his daughter. Nell pretty much summed it up when she'd warned him that that was what parenting was all about.

Janelle always seemed to have plenty of time to accompany Dan to a swim meet or football game. When she couldn't, Jackson was safe enough to send him off on his own. What the hell was he busting his butt for? He had enough money to retire tomorrow if he wanted. Tom guessed he didn't really want to badly enough and not quite yet.

He leaned back in his chair, hands behind his head, and checked the clock. Almost time for Janelle's call. He was going to miss Jackson this weekend, and they'd talked daily on the phone to assuage the disappointment.

He tried to visualize her stretched out on the big brass bed as they talked, even though he knew she was sitting at the kitchen table. He let her sighs wash over him, reminding him of the way she sighed in his arms, her wordless approval. He listened to the endless details of life in a small town and tried to imagine how it would be different if he was there.

He and Tippy had spent a few weekends in Jackson as if to test the theory, and it had been great, with one big exception. A little time alone with Janelle wasn't enough. Neither of them were content with kisses, and they were interrupted just often enough to make them realize that a house with two teens wasn't conducive to privacy. His only consolation was the longing he read in Janelle's eyes. He was sure it was reflected by his own.

The phone rang and Tom knocked the script to the floor in his haste to answer it. His hello was breathless.

"I love the roses. Thank you." Her voice was dreamy, as though just mentioning the roses conjured up a hundred romantic thoughts.

"I wanted you to think of me, even though I can't be there."

"The smell is wonderful. I keep carrying them around the house with me. I like them best in the bedroom, I think. They make the whole room brighter."

Tom was quiet a moment, visualizing the red blossoms on her pillow, where he wanted to be, caressing her face with velvety softness.

Janelle obviously misinterpreted the silence. "Are you busy? I tried calling before, but the line was busy. If you're working, you can call me back later."

"I'm not doing a thing." Tom turned his back on the pile of scripts and promptly forgot them. "Tippy called before, complaining about her math teacher. What's Dan doing this weekend?" Tom was toying with the idea of inviting them to Chicago. He wondered why they hadn't thought of it before.

"He has a scout camp-out. He leaves right after school tomorrow and he'll be back sometime late Sunday."

Tom sat up straight. "Dan's going to be away?" The question was rhetorical, and he continued without a pause. "Janelle, honey, why don't you come down here for the weekend?"

Janelle was silent for a long moment. "Tom, I'd love it." Again a pause. "But what if Dan needs something?"

Tom fought a surge of exasperation. She had to stop trying to be all things to all people. While he was trying to figure out a more diplomatic way to phrase that, Janelle spoke again.

"I guess he could call Ned or Kathy if he needed something or the weather turned bad."

"He could do that. It really wouldn't hurt him to know that you need a life of your own. But, listen, it's up to you." He was standing now, fists clenched, willing her to come.

"Okay, I'd really love to." She paused. "I can't wait, Tom." He could all but hear her consider the ramifications of the weekend. "But what will I tell everyone here?"

His answer was prompt. "That you're spending the weekend in decadent seclusion with me."

"Well, I may go for something a little more discreet." She sounded amused and elated. She cleared her throat and tried to sound dignified. "Something like, I have to come to Chicago for a meeting—"

"Nell, you can tell them anything you want. All I want to know is how soon you can get here."

The residue of Chicago's Friday night rush hour was just what she needed to keep her mind off the rest of the weekend. Concentrating on the traffic weaving in and around her car allowed little time to daydream.

Janelle was sure this was the right decision. She'd even stopped at a drugstore and taken care of birth control. But now she was filled with those age-old fears. Now that they were going to be lovers she was afraid she wouldn't measure up. She was afraid she was too old, not pretty enough, not experienced enough. She wanted desperately to please him, and for once her much-valued common sense had been left behind. This wasn't the weekend for it, but a small dose here and there would have helped still the butterflies.

Traffic thinned as she left the interstate and found her way to Tom's exclusive suburban neighborhood. She didn't like it any more this time than she had on her first visit. It embodied most of what she disliked about city life, people who separated themselves into exclusive little groups whether they were rich or poor, isolating themselves further by the pace of their lives and the drive for more.

Tom had bought into it at one point. His giant, impersonal house was proof of that. But somehow this house didn't fit with the Tom Wineski she loved. It was one of the mysteries she wanted to solve this weekend.

As she pulled to a stop in the circular driveway, Janelle flipped off the radio on the final notes of Carly Simon's "Anticipation." It just about summed up the last few weeks. That song had always been a favorite, but now she was ready to move on to a different theme. She grabbed her suitcase and the bag of fresh vegetables. Balancing them in one hand, she rang the bell.

Did she look all right? Maybe she should have checked her hair and makeup one more time? Her black and white dress was brand-new and perfect, with three big buttons sweeping on the diagonal to the wrap-around waist. The moment Tom opened the door, she knew none of that mattered.

She noticed his black pants and cotton shirt, but they registered in an automatic visual sweep. What she really saw was a smile that reached his eyes and drew her into an embrace without the slightest physical contact.

Tom stood aside and waved her in with a courtly gesture. "Either you left earlier than you said or you broke every speed limit between here and Jackson."

"A little of both." The conversation was prosaic, but they were communicating on another level as well.

Janelle's smile matched Tom's, acknowledging that they'd both waited so long for this.

"How was the Friday traffic?"

"It all seems horrendous to me. Three cars waiting at the drive-up bank window is a traffic jam in Jackson, but I managed."

Tom took Janelle's bag and the vegetables and left them on a chair in the front hall. "Did Dan get off okay?"

"Oh, sure, just the usual hunt for all the right gear at the last minute. Honestly, we've lived in that house long enough for him to know where everything is blindfolded, but it's still a big production every time he gets ready for one of these things."

The conversation continued, but so much more was said by the twist of the head, a touch of the hand, a secret smile.

Before the trivia was exhausted, they walked through the house to a book-lined room overlooking the garden. A mound of pillows lay between the chintz-covered sofa and the fireplace, where a fire burned with the sedate precision of gas logs. The room was welcoming, even though it seemed more like a set for *Masterpiece Theatre* than someone's family room.

There was a bottle of wine on a butler's tray, and Tom poured Janelle a glass as she settled on the floor close to the fire with her back against the couch. Wine was the last thing she needed. She already felt as though champagne was bubbling in her veins—light-headed and smiling as though she knew the world's best-kept secret. And like the feeling that accompanies the euphoria of a wine-induced haze, a little part of her was afraid it wasn't as perfect as it seemed.

Tom leaned against the fireplace mantel. "It's hard to believe."

Janelle was willing to take the cue. "What is?"

"It's hard to believe that all my most fantastic dreams are about to come true, and all I can do is talk about the weather."

Her laughter was a spontaneous agreement and a welcome vent for some of the emotion charging the room. "I suppose I could walk over there and wrap my body around you and tease you into a frenzy, but don't you think that would be rushing things?"

It was Tom's turn to laugh. "Hell no, you know it's all we've been thinking about for the last few weeks."

With a wistful smile Janelle agreed. "Since one very memorable picnic."

Tom crossed the room and sat down next to her, drawing Janelle into the circle of his arm. They both leaned back against the couch and stared at the flames. It felt so familiar. The sense of belonging was so strong that she knew it would be all right. In fact, it would be great.

Welcome replaced hesitation. Happiness replaced anxiety. Promise replaced doubt.

She lay her head back on his arm resting behind her and looked into his eyes. "You are the most wonderful man I know."

The words vibrated against her mouth as Tom traced her lips with his tongue. His kiss was a soft hello that grew in demand as passion drew them together. He threaded his hands through her hair, drawing her closer as he tasted her mouth with a sensuality that drew its own response, a soft moan of pleasure, a single shiver of emotion.

Janelle lost herself in the swirl of feeling that bound them together. The tantalizing memory of all those other kisses was embodied in this beginning that would end in fulfillment.

Their lips parted but remained only a breath apart. Janelle smiled and touched her lips to his. "I bet this house has at least four extra bedrooms." Her voice was low and teasing.

"Five."

He breathed the number into her ear and followed it with a like number of kisses along her cheek. "And I've imagined us in every one. I've even imagined us here, planned the scene and written the script."

Janelle sat a little straighter. The first two buttons of Tom's shirt were undone, so she started on the third. Her fingers were steady, but so sensitized she could feel the beat of his heart as she slipped the small button through the hole. She was working on the fourth when she looked up. "Am I doing this right or do I need further direction?"

His smile was all the encouragement she needed, and she hurried the last few buttons. She wanted to touch him, to feel him close to her, to revel in each of the moves she'd anticipated for so long.

She slid her hands up his chest, enjoying the feel of muscle that rippled at his slightest move. She let her lips take the same path, leaving a trail of light liquid kisses as she tasted the slightly salty flavor of his skin. Then she pressed against him in a sinuous invitation that Tom responded to immediately.

In one deft movement, the thick carpet became their bed. Tom moved with tantalizing slowness as he imitated Janelle's actions. The three large buttons on her dress were easily unfastened, and the clothes discarded with a disregard born of their single-minded goal.

The room was warm and darkening with dusk, and the crackling of the fire matched their sparking passion. Tom and Janelle were in tune with each other and the elemental sensations that embodied their narrowing world.

Janelle wound her arms tightly around Tom's neck, drawing him in complete contact with her body. The hardness of his manhood pressed into her, waiting for a welcoming movement that was impossible to deny, yet all the sweeter for waiting.

Tom coaxed her thighs apart with soft touches that moved closer and closer to intimate contact in a teasing rhythm that her body responded to with a cadence of its own. He slid his hand over her most sensitive spots with gentle caresses that promised and tempted, sharing just a part of the intensity of fulfillment. With a whispered moan of sensual demand, Janelle arched her body, and Tom entered her with a single smooth thrust. They remained completely still for a moment, Janelle adjusting to the unaccustomed sensation with a smile of pleasure. Tom moved slowly at first, teasing her with long, slow strokes that brought anticipation to new heights. Janelle lay still until the tension was unbearable. With a moan of surrender she met his movements, blending her body to the rhythm of his. Gradually the tempo increased until a single burst of pleasure swept through them, so intense that it bound them together for a forever moment that was magically selfish and selfless.

They were completely still once again, each treasuring the physical response that expressed their emotions so completely. They lay in each other's arms, eyes closed, until the slight heat of the fire wasn't enough warmth. It was completely dark now, the room lit only by the flames of the fire.

Tom made no move to turn on a light. Instead, he reached up and pulled a lightweight comforter from the end of the couch and draped it over both of them. They moved to the sofa and sat wrapped in each other's arms, watching the fire, savoring the intimacy.

It was entirely too early to go to bed, but neither commented on the hour. With her dress draped over her shoulders and shoes in hand, Janelle followed Tom up the circular staircase in the corner of the library. Tom's bedroom was directly above, with a similar fireplace, this one with real logs. The only other pieces of furniture in the room were a bed and two end tables.

She watched Tom move to light the fire and marveled at the beauty of his body, his broad shoulders tapering to a trim waist and those long, lean legs. He seemed thin in clothes, almost too thin, but out of them he was perfect. Far more perfect than she.

He turned and watched her nestle against the pillows, knowing exactly what was on her mind. There was only one way to convince her that for him she was the most beautiful woman in the world. As he crossed the floor, Tom never took his eyes from her. He stared at her with an intensity that wouldn't allow her to look away. He sat on the bed beside her and bent to kiss her neck and seduce her into a sexual lethargy.

"You have the most responsive body, Janelle," he whispered to her as he traced the ridge of her ear with his tongue, then teased her earlobe with his teeth. "I know I can kiss you here." He touched a spot at the base of her neck and he felt her shiver. "And in an instant you'll want me as much as I want you."

He stopped and stretched his body next to hers, touching her just enough so that the hunger never left. "Right now, Janelle, it wouldn't matter how old we were, what we looked like. Nothing matters but the wanting."

He bent his head and teased her breast with soft circles of pressure and then her mouth with harsher demand. "Remember, Janelle. Nothing else matters."

She opened her eyes and smiled at him, silently accepting his words. He smiled back and lowered his lips to her mouth, teasing it open with soft sweeps of his tongue.

He traced the line of her body with his fingertips, finally resting them tantalizing inches from the heart of her need. As he gently kissed her mouth, he continued to stroke her until she arched her body with eloquent demand, urging on the edge of fulfillment.

She was a quiet lover—soft sweet sighs and eager moans, but no words, just total giving and sharing.

He took his mouth from hers and watched her face as he eased himself inside her. He smiled as her eyes flew open, and an accompanying cry of pleasure told him how well he'd read her needs. Janelle took control for a moment, her body

beginning an urgent movement beneath his. He slowed her
with his hands on her hips, savoring the approaching burst
of pleasure.

As his tempo matched hers, he lost himself in the primitive union. He didn't want it to end. The physical act would
culminate in the same incredible surge of pleasure and
power, but the wanting would go on and on. He couldn't see
an end to it and didn't want to.

There was little sleep that night. They lived their fantasies by the light of the moon and the stars. They dozed, then
shared their dreams. At three in the morning, they remembered supper and invaded the kitchen for champagne,
cheese and bread. By first light, they finally fell soundly
asleep.

Janelle awoke first. Tom slept facing her, his hand resting lightly on her shoulder. She moved a little and kissed
each finger until he smiled in his sleep. Moving a little closer,
she watched the smile grow and knew that he wasn't asleep
any longer. With his eyes still closed he murmured, "I've
created a monster—and I love every minute of it."

It was a day to treasure. A blustery rain gave them the
perfect excuse to stay inside, and they made omelets for
brunch—Tom's spicy with salsa and chili, Janelle's full of
sautéed vegetables.

They watched old movies on the VCR, and Tom recited
his favorite scenes by heart. Then, while Janelle cooked
dinner, Tom serenaded her with his banjo. He promised to
show her the video of his Grammy appearance, then pretended he couldn't find it. Janelle let him get away with the
fib, but surreptitiously slipped the tape into the player when
he went to get the wine left behind in the kitchen. By the
time he returned, she was engrossed in his performance.

As the tape rewound, she stood up and crossed to where
he was standing. She slipped her arms around his waist. "If
you ever get tired of acting, there's obviously another way
you can earn your living."

"Playing the banjo?" There was a hopeful note in his
voice that made Janelle giggle. Tom's kiss caught the giggle

and smothered it. The laughter never left their kiss and the two of them shared the happiness that swept through them with all the force of the sun on a cloudless day.

A day to treasure. The phrase echoed through Janelle's happiness as they walked down the hall to the bedroom. No matter how long it lasted, this sharing was worth all the uncertainty in their future.

They slept late once again. This time the phone woke them, and Tom was thoroughly disgruntled. "Nell, I'm sorry. I left a message for Harris to cancel this mall appearance I was supposed to make today. He was in L.A. and no one in that whole damn office knows how to use a phone unless he tells them."

Janelle smiled at his ill humor. Going to a mall and watching a group of teenagers harass Tom wasn't exactly the way she'd envisioned spending the last of her time with him, but she wasn't about to be selfish. The last twenty-four hours had put her on top of the world and ready to be more than just a little magnanimous. "How about if I come with you? We could find presents for the kids. Maybe we'll even get back in time for a swim."

Coaxing Tom out of his poor humor took longer than she anticipated, and they had to rush through dressing and brunch in order to be ready when the limousine arrived.

Tom looked different. Gone were the casual jeans and cotton shirts she was used too. Now he was dressed all in black leather and was King all the way.

"I guess we should forget about shopping." She hadn't meant to sound disappointed. Tom didn't need a petulant companion to add to his responsibilities. She was determined to handle this like an adult.

"Why's that? We'll have plenty of time after." Tom pulled her into his arms and whispered, "If I'd known you like shopping so much, I wouldn't have insisted on that shower together."

She stared straight into his eyes, forgetting the costume, only seeing the man she loved and had made love to for half the night. "I wouldn't have traded that shower for all the stores in America."

He kissed her quickly. "Just checking." Tom let her slip out of his arms, but kept a firm hold of her hand as he led her out the door to the waiting limousine. "So, why won't we be able to shop?"

"Oh, it's just that I always forget the recognition factor. There'll be a mob following you everywhere." Really, it was something she would have to get used to. It was a part of his life.

He brushed her concern aside. "We'll work something out. You know, Nell, it comes with the package. It isn't going to change anytime soon." He watched her carefully.

She leaned over and kissed him. "You're right. I was just thinking the same thing. I guess I better get used to it." She slid closer to him and sat in the protection of his arm, holding tight to their dreamworld even as it faded away.

"Actually, this is one privilege I'd have no trouble getting used to," she said, looking around at the limousine and all its accoutrements of success.

"You like this?" Tom's voice echoed his surprise.

"Actually, I could do without all the doodads, but I've forgotten everything I ever knew about city driving. I like letting someone else worry about it."

"And I like driving so much that this is no fun for me at all." He stopped abruptly, then seemed to make a conscious decision to go on. "You know, I think of this thing as a sort of ego machine. I get in here and leave home behind, and by the time I get to the studio, the mall, wherever, I'm not me anymore but that money-making machine that means so much to everyone but you."

"Maybe the secret is having someone to share it with to remind you that the real you is loved and valued."

"It sure helps." He smiled at her, but his expression was unreadable. "God knows, Nell, just having you near makes the whole world a little more sane."

They were met by Harris and a couple of mall officials who managed to act businesslike, despite their awe. Tom took the time to introduce Janelle to the men, and they all responded politely without any obvious curiosity. Feeling just a little more relaxed, she walked beside Tom as the group made its way to the executive offices while listening to Harris discuss the appearance.

"Just a half hour. That's all the time we agreed to and no autographs."

Tom rolled his eyes and shook his head. "Listen, let's be realistic, Harris." He turned to the mall manager. "I'll give you an hour with half the time for autographs, if you can fix it so Janelle and I can go to that small shop the Handicap Guild runs. We want to pick up a couple of presents."

He gave Janelle a wink and a nod as the manager agreed. She smiled back. At least he was trying. What more could she ask?

The next hour was everything she'd imagined it would be. The mall security people broke up the gathering just as the girls started to beg for kisses. Tom signed the last autograph, waved a hasty goodbye and exited the stage into the narrow hall leading to the executive offices. He stayed a few minutes chatting with the manager and spent a few minutes longer in conversation with Harris.

The couple running the Handicap Guild Shop were thrilled to meet him. For Janelle, it was the highlight of the day. Tom let the blind girl manning the register "read" his face with her fingers and commiserated with the clerk on crutches. His own football injuries had given them a common ground. When they left, laden with their purchases, there was a long line waiting to get into the small shop. It was a quiet kind of goodwill that made Janelle love him all the more.

She hadn't counted on sharing the ride home with Harris. What she really wanted was to get Tom out of that slick jacket and his King personality. Instead, they sat next to each other, facing his manager, who rode on the jump seat. Janelle listened as the two men discussed a list of possible promotional appearances and how they might help Tom in his upcoming contract negotiations. The drive seemed interminable, their last two hours together slipping away under a barrage of business.

Janelle was relieved to see the house and that worried her even more. When *that* monstrosity started to look good, she feared she was losing touch with reality.

They were barely through the door when Tom pushed it shut, then backed Janelle against it. He didn't touch her, but put his hands on either side of her head, effectively trapping her.

"Barely two hours, door-to-door. That wasn't too bad was it?" He was arrogant, in command, and very much like King. She could sense the excitement, maybe even tension in him. Why did she feel exhausted? She shook her head in response to his question, still trying to repress her feelings.

He shrugged out of his leather jacket and urged Janelle down the hall toward the kitchen. "There's something I want to talk to you about. I thought about it most of the way home. I hardly heard a word Harris was saying. I sure hope I didn't agree to anything too outlandish."

Janelle moved down the hall with him, very much at his command. She was swept along by his exuberant mood, not sharing it, but unwilling to squelch it. He propped her on the stool by the counter and took her hand.

"Nell, you know how much it means to me to have you here, as a part of my life. Now that we know exactly what a dynamite thing we've got, why waste any more time? How long would it take you to pack up your stuff and move down here? The house has plenty of room for Dan, and I'm sure he could go to the same school as Tippy. We could go up to Jackson as often as you want. Sounds like a great idea, right?"

Why couldn't the man take it one step at a time? She was afraid to trust her instincts and believe in fairy tales, afraid to ask for something he might not be willing to give.

Emotional chaos and physical fatigue made reasonable thought impossible. Janelle took refuge in anger. "Let me get this straight. You want me to leave Jackson and everything I'm familiar with and move down here with you?" She tried to calm down, forcing herself to relax her clenched fists and even manage a grimace that might pass for a smile.

Tom nodded. "I take it the idea doesn't appeal to you." He might have meant the smile to be placating—Janelle interpreted it as patronizing.

"Not really. I like my life-style; it's important to me. I may not make as much money as you, but even you have to admit there's a lot to recommend life in Jackson." She sat up straight, not shouting, but speaking with a quiet indignation.

"Is it because you're afraid of moving back to the city?"

"No." The single word carried a wealth of exasperation. "I have interests, too. I have a son I want to raise my way. I don't even like this monstrosity of a house." She waved all those dislikes away. "What I don't like most of all is that you're so used to being the focal point of everything, and you're too selfish to even consider what I want."

"Now just a minute, Janelle." He pushed off the wall and followed her as she walked down the hall. She stopped at the foot of the stairs and turned to face him once again. "I'm selfish? Selfish because I want you close to me?"

She shrugged her shoulders, conceding the ambiguity.

"Besides, Nell, selfish is a two-way street. I can't change my life right now. I've got contracts and commitments and a lot of people demanding things from me. Can't you see that?"

"Of course I can. The problem is that you can't see that I have commitments, too. It's going to take time for both of us to learn to balance them all. I guess it's not romantic, but it *is* realistic."

Maybe they needed some time apart. Maybe it was time to leave. Time to get away from the incredible physical desire and think about this whole situation objectively. She tried for a conciliatory tone. "I don't want to argue about this, Tom. Can't you just accept the fact that I'm not ready to talk about this, and I'm certainly not ready for any more big changes in my life?"

She watched as his jaw tightened for a moment. Then he nodded. Maybe the line about selfishness had hit home. "I probably should be going. I wanted to get home before Dan got back from his camp-out, otherwise he'll just drop everything and forget about it until—"

Tom interrupted, "I think we need to work this out now, Janelle."

"What I need is to be alone for a while. I'm not ready for this, and I wish you would accept that and let me go."

"All right." He held up his hand as if to cut off another diatribe. "But I'm coming to Jackson next weekend. I hope you have some answers by then. Think about it on the way home. That two-hour drive should be good for something."

It was hardly the end to the weekend Janelle had envisioned. She concentrated on the traffic and turned to a call-in talk show, losing herself in other people's problems. She would start thinking when she was good and ready.

Nine

Tom tried to concentrate on the group of children on stage, but a small-town production of *The Sound of Music* wasn't going to hold his attention for long. He attempted to pick out Kathy's kids in the group of Von Trapp children singing, then gave up. Tonight the flat Wisconsin voices all sounded the same. Janelle sat beside him, all her attention apparently focused on the play. With a sidelong glance, Tom decided she wasn't paying any more attention than he was. Her face remained expressionless, not reacting at all to the sentimentality on stage.

He'd noticed how quiet she was within minutes of their arrival, and he found her silence disconcerting. He hadn't called once this past week, and he'd expected her to be brimming with conversation. At first he decided she was letting the two kids have center stage. Fall Fest weekend was the highlight of the season and promised more activities than the small town generated the rest of the year. Dan insisted on reviewing all the activities as soon as Tom and Tippy arrived. Janelle had joined them at the kitchen table, but sat in silence while the two youngsters discussed the merits of the various events.

When Janelle had remained unusually quiet on the drive to the theater and even after the kids had gone to sit with their friends, Tom felt the first stirrings of fear. Not physical fear. He couldn't remember three times in his life when he'd ever felt afraid that way. This was the gut-wrenching, emotional kind of fear. He was afraid that Janelle was getting ready for goodbye. He kept trying to tell himself he was overreacting, that there was a simple explanation for her withdrawal.

She was exhausted. It had been a hectic week for her, helping to organize a number of events, plus keeping up with her usual routine. As hard as he tried to convince himself it was simple fatigue, he was afraid his first guess had been right. She wanted out.

Giving in to his most melancholy speculation, he tried to visualize a life without her.

Empty. It had been that way before, but then he hadn't known what he was missing. He'd gone through the motions, ignoring the loneliness, hoping that when he had custody of Tippy the feeling would disappear. Tippy had helped, but it was Janelle that was the touchstone for all the warmth in his life, and it would be worth almost anything to keep her there. Ever since that confrontation on her back porch, the fire had been evident. It still was and it wouldn't fade, he was sure of that. Now he was close to blowing it all because of a well-intentioned suggestion that they move in together. The idea seemed as natural to him as holding hands and making love, but apparently Janelle didn't feel the same. God knows he hadn't meant to sound selfish, although he knew he'd been impulsive.

He shifted in his seat, trying to ignore the restlessness that had ruined his week. He knew they belonged together and was frustrated at every moment they were apart. Why did Janelle have to make it so difficult? Tom slid down in the chair, completely ignoring the show and considering his options.

By the time the final curtain fell, he was a little closer to a solution. First on his list was to get her to smile. Step two was to remind her what they had and how good it was. He would take step three, a quiet conversation, only when the time was right.

The small school theater was filled with appreciative friends, relatives and parents. The crowd moved toward the exits slowly, taking advantage of the close quarters to get one more close look at the man who had become a familiar face around town. With a protective arm around Janelle, Tom worked his way up the aisle.

It was clear that Fall Fest weekend in Jackson left precious little opportunity for quiet conversation. Patience had never been his strong suit, but he promised himself once again to wait until just the right moment. One thing he'd learned last weekend was how little Janelle liked surprises.

He hugged her close for a moment, hoping a little part of the love he felt for her would penetrate the trivial conversation around them.

Tom unlocked the Porsche and held the door. Before she slipped in, he stopped her with a touch.

"You know, we could just not show up at the cast party." He smiled and raised his eyebrows.

Janelle smiled back, the first real smile he'd seen all evening. "There's nothing I'd like more than some time alone with you." She paused and sighed. "But they'll be really disappointed if we don't stop by."

"I guess our disappointment doesn't count for much."

"It's called being mature, responsible adults." She chanted the words in the tone all teens associate with parents.

She shook her head in laughter when Tom responded, "It sounds like garbage to me."

He hurried over to the driver's side, mentally giving himself a point. Step one was accomplished—she was smiling again.

Kathy's yard was festooned with Christmas lights, adding to the party atmosphere. It was a warm evening, and the overflow from the party, mostly teens, had spilled out into the front yard where the kids were gyrating to music blaring from an impressive boom-box propped on the front-porch railing.

Tom parked the car at the end of a long row of vehicles. "Wow, it's a good thing they live in the country. That's loud enough to rival most nightclubs."

Janelle slipped her hand in the crook of his arm. "Kathy and Ned have one party a year. This is the official start of Fall Fest for the family and half the rest of town, too."

"And you thought we'd be missed if we didn't show up?" Tom stopped halfway up the driveway. He looked skeptical.

"Tom, you saw the way the crowd gathered round you at the theater. You're familiar to them now, but you're hardly in the local-yokel class. Half these people are probably here to see you."

Tom's shoulders sagged and Janelle patted his arm. "Look at it as your final initiation. We won't stay long, only a half hour."

A sense of déjà vu struck Tom. He shook his head, his voice petulant. "You sound like Harris. We'll be here for hours."

Janelle stepped away and shook her head. "And you sound like a grumpy child."

With a little tug, he pulled her into his arms. "I know what would make me feel better." She wound her arms around his neck. "And it would sort of give us something to look forward to."

Janelle didn't need any coaxing. She leaned into him and kissed him with a desperate longing that stirred Tom's fears anew. It wasn't goodbye, but almost as worrisome. She kissed him as if they had no future. Tom leaned back against the fence, pulling her into closer contact, determined to change the mood. His kiss was a promise, his mouth caressing her lips, his tongue branding her mouth, his hands cradling her with intimate familiarity. He was convinced the chemistry was still there, would always be there if he had his way. He hoped he'd convinced Janelle as well.

It didn't take long for a crowd to gather around Tom. Janelle wasn't inclined to follow, but sat on the kitchen counter chatting with a couple of women she knew from her work with the swim team. Actually she was listening. The other two were doing all the talking.

"I mean, I think this is going to be the best Fall Fest ever. The play's finally over, the beer tent has plenty of brew on tap and having Tom Wineski turning up every now and then really makes it exciting." She turned her attention to Janelle. "How'd you ever talk him into showing up, Janelle?"

Janelle thought of a dozen answers, but opted for diplomacy. "Tippy has friends here and they both really enjoy visiting."

The other woman spoke up, her voice disbelieving. "Sure he does. The guy can snap his fingers and have anything—or anyone—he wants. And you're telling me Jackson is first choice on his list of things to do?"

"Maybe it would appeal for a few weeks," her friend chimed in, "but the novelty's bound to wear off soon."

Janelle excused herself and elbowed her way out the back door. Her meager store of good humor had been decimated by the twosome, and she walked down the back steps toward a couple of lawn chairs scattered around the backyard.

They were only asking questions everyone else asked. How could she explain? Jackson gave Tom a taste of normalcy, an idea of what it was like to live a conventional life untouched by the distortions of fame. It was as novel to him as his life-style was to the folks of Jackson.

Janelle thought about the woman's comment about the novelty of the situation. That was what worried Janelle. She wondered if it had happened already. Was Tom's suggestion that she move to Chicago his way of saying that he'd had enough of small-town life? If that was so, how long before he'd had enough of her?

An overwhelming emotional fatigue swept through her. The week had been an emotional seesaw, leaving her tired and heartsore. On the upside she remembered the weekend they'd shared and longed for more. On the downward swoop was the absurdity of Tom's demand that she move.

Now that he was there, the ride was even more frenetic. One minute she would be lost in a world of doubt and the next swept high by a smile, a glance or a kiss. The doubt would disappear, but could a whole life be built on a smile? Was it worth the risk?

She liked her life in Jackson, liked its predictability, the routine. She could trust what she knew. If she changed her life and tried to build a world with Tom, she would have to start all over again, with no defenses, and no guarantees.

With a snort of disgust, she pushed the conflict to a corner of her mind and headed back to the house. She wasn't going to resolve it here in Kathy's backyard; maybe tomorrow, after the polka party, or if she was really gutsy, after the parade. For now, she was determined to have a good time.

Setting the two soda cans on the table, Tom settled into a comfortable position in the rocking chair he now considered his own. He closed his eyes and rocked slowly, listening to the even timbre of Janelle's voice as she hurried the phone conversation along.

After the noise of the parade, the relative quiet was welcome. Now was the time for that third phase of his three-point program. Janelle seemed more relaxed. They'd enjoyed the parade and the camaraderie of the small-town celebration.

He rocked back in his chair, organizing the thoughts that had been crowding his mind since the play. He really liked it in Jackson. He could understand why people stayed. He could live here. It wouldn't be that hard to give up the Chicago house and settle here if it meant that much to Janelle.

It would be good for Tippy, too, but it would be one hell of a commute. Maybe he would try to work a plane into his next contract.

He was rehearsing opening lines when the back door snapped shut.

"That was Irene checking to see if we saw Tippy and Dan in the parade." She sank into her chair and leaned her head back on the cushioned headrest.

Tom popped the tab on his can of soda and took a long swallow. "I thought the kids looked great in those turn-of-the-century costumes. They were prefect for riding in the classic car division."

Janelle turned and looked at him. "Irene made them years ago. Every few years another set of grandkids gets to wear them. It is kind of neat, isn't it?"

He tried to gauge her mood. Was now the right time? He watched as she rocked, her eyes closed. No, he decided. She was more relaxed, smiling a little, but obviously tired. No matter how much it nagged at him, he would have to wait a little longer. He settled back in the chair across the table from her and tried for casual conversation.

"So how would you rate this year's parade?"

Janelle yawned. "It was okay, I guess."

Tom didn't give up. "How did it compare to the last few?" She rocked back in her chair and propped her feet on the railing. "You want me to rate the parade? On a scale of ten, I'd say it was about a six."

Tom was indignant. "It was better than that, Janelle. The program said there were four bands this year. That's an all-time record. And according to Ned, eliminating the prize-winning milk cows speeded things up a good bit. The only real lag I could see was between the float with the dancing corn husks and the group from the juggling club."

Janelle was laughing now and getting into the spirit. "Those jugglers *always* hold things up. The beginners are forever dropping the clubs. One year the entire parade went by while Tim Sweringen tried to retrieve a club that had rolled into the sewer."

Tom had never heard of the kid, but he wasn't about to stop now. "Good old Tim. I didn't see him in the juggling group this year. As a matter of fact, I didn't see him at all."

"Tom, he was darn hard to miss. He's moved on to the high-school marching band." Now she couldn't stop laughing and managed to get out a sentence between gasps. "He was the one who kept going in the wrong direction on their precision turns." She controlled her laughter and reached over to touch him. "Did it all seem hopelessly hokey to you?"

He took her hand and held it tight. "It was fun. Sure it was corny. But it was like we were all part of the show, even the folks on the sidelines. Believe me, you don't get that feel at the Rose Bowl Parade. I liked it a lot. It's definitely in a class by itself."

Now that she was smiling at him again, another thought entered his mind, or rather, it didn't so much enter his mind as invade his senses. "How long before the kids get back?" He tried to sound casual, but he could tell from Janelle's expression that she was all but reading his thoughts.

"They're going to walk around the midway in their costumes and see if they can get any free tickets for rides. Then they're going to meet us at the food hall for supper."

"In about two hours, right?"

They stood up at the same time.

Janelle watched him with a perfectly straight face. "I've got a whole album of pictures from the last few parades. Would you like to see them? I think they're up in my room."

Tom followed her into the house. "Do you think we have enough time?"

Janelle paused at the bottom of the steps. "Depends on how long we spend looking at the pictures." She turned and raced up the steps, Tom close behind.

As she entered the room, Janelle flipped on the fan and reached up to pull the pins from her hair. Tom watched her for a moment, then grabbed her hands from behind. He held them with one hand while he played maid, pulling the last of the pins out with agonizing slowness. Janelle stood docilely as he reached for the zipper on the back of her dress and the limp cotton slipped to her waist.

With both hands still holding hers captive, he turned her toward him, crushing her naked breasts against his chest. Despite his shirt between them, he felt her nipples harden in response. He moved his hands to fondle the hard rosy crown of her breast, and Janelle reached up on tiptoe, moving intimately against him as she fitted her body to his and her mouth to his lips.

In between kisses she undressed him and pulled the covers back on her brass bed. Tom eased her down on the mattress. The cotton of the sheets felt cool on his naked skin, and the oscillating fan blew regular whispers of air across them.

Where he would have been slow, she was impatient.

"Don't make me wait, Tom, please. It's been too long," she murmured, accompanying her words with caresses that heightened his need.

It didn't take much persuasion for him to increase the tempo of their lovemaking. Her hand directed his entry, her hips arched in welcome. Lost in a world of sensual pleasure, the tide of feeling swept over them. It had been a long week. Seven days' worth of erotic dreams were played out in a few tempestuous minutes.

They lay silent for a time, each overwhelmed by the scope of their need and response.

"Sometimes there are just too many people around."

Tom kissed her cheek. "I know. The parade was lots of fun, but it doesn't even run a close second to spending time alone with you."

Janelle's long sigh of agreement disappeared in a yawn.

"I know how tired you must be, honey. How about a little nap?"

Janelle smiled. "How can you make something as innocent as a nap sound sinful."

"Not me, Nell, that's your mind at work."

Janelle's chuckle of agreement disappeared in one more yawn. A moment later she was asleep.

Tom listened to the quiet rhythm of her breathing. Settling back on the pillow, he relaxed. He dozed off, watching the soft vulnerability of her face, wondering if her eyes were green or blue when she slept.

When they both opened their eyes at the same moment Janelle decided the afternoon paper hitting the front door had been their alarm.

Tom leaned closer so their bodies were touching. "Your eyes are blue when you sleep."

"No, they're not. My eyes are a sort of washed-out, hazelly green."

"Most of the time, but whenever we're this close together—" he pressed against her to demonstrate "—the hazel disappears and a lovely blue takes its place. Which do you suppose is their true color?"

Janelle smiled and turned from her side to lie on her back. It didn't lessen the contact, but rather fitted them more comfortably together. How could heaven come this close to earth, she wondered? She smiled at him. "Should we try for a scientific explanation on eyes and eye color?"

"Not really. Maybe I'll conduct a little experiment of my own." He leaned over and kissed her with a passionate conviction that left her breathless, blue-eyed and hungry. "Janelle." He lay back with his head on his hand, passion in check. "I want to talk to you about something."

She smiled in anticipation, intrigued by his tone.

"Janelle, those roses say it all." He nodded toward the bouquet of red roses he'd brought along this weekend. "I love you." He nodded his head as if the words sounded just right and repeated the declaration with a kind of wondering conviction that made Janelle's smile grow broader.

"You're sure you're not swept up in the feeling of the moment?" She wasn't really skeptical, just teasing him a bit.

"No. I've felt this way for days, weeks, maybe even months, and I couldn't wait another minute to tell you."

He pulled her closer once again, but stared into space as he spoke. "About what happened last weekend. I know now how you feel about moving to Chicago." He paused a moment. "You haven't changed your mind, have you?"

The negative shake of her head was as much answer as Tom thought he would get. Then she spoke. "I've thought about it a lot and I can't say I've changed my mind, weakened a little, but not changed it."

He didn't seem distressed by it and continued. "The fact remains, I love you and want to be with you as much as possible."

Janelle was touched by the declaration, but a flicker of alarm trickled through the aura of sensuality. He had another plan. Janelle tried to move and was about to speak when Tom's hold tightened.

"Honey, please, listen. My contract comes up for renewal soon. I was going to let Harris and my agent handle it, but I've been thinking that if I could make some changes that would give us more time together, now is the time to do it."

"Like what sort of changes?" She angled her body away from him and tried to repress the skepticism that was destroying her mood.

"I thought I could set it up so I could move here."

"How could you do that?" Now she was surprised, incredulous. "I mean, Tom, you have a lot of people at your command, but even they can't fix it so you can be two places at once."

As he explained about the plane, or maybe a helicopter, Janelle listened and the skepticism disappeared. She wasn't sure whether to laugh or be practical. "Tom, that sounds good in theory, but you'd be exhausted in two months. You'd never have any time for Tippy." Much less me, she added to herself. "I don't think it would work."

She regretted her wholesale rejection of the idea almost immediately, but couldn't think of a way to soften her reaction. While she was still struggling for something more neutral, Tom sat up, threw back the covers and began to look for his clothes. "You know, Nell, if I didn't know better, I'd think you didn't want this to work. We both know that we have to find some kind of compromise. It seems to me that you aren't even willing to try to make it work."

Janelle thought of her week's worth of restless nights. She'd thought long and hard, trying to find a solution. She hadn't come up with any, but his weren't any better. "But your suggestions aren't realistic."

"What the hell's so unrealistic about one of us moving. It's the only way we can live together. I'm not into commuter relationships."

"Be reasonable, Tom. That's what we'd have if you tried to live here and commute to Chicago. It's a two-hour trip by car and you never know what your schedule is." Janelle sat upright and tried not to sound cynical.

Dressed in his pants, he stood at the foot of the bed, hands on hips. "All right, you don't like that. How about this?" He sounded as though he was negotiating a contract. "I quit the Chicago setup. No more King, no more acting, I'll dump the whole thing. I move up here and go into business with Ned. He could use some financing on that second store he wants to buy. Then we could be together without any complications."

Janelle heard the anger in his voice. The how's-that-for-sacrifice tone. "You wouldn't last six months. There's a whole part of your personality that needs the bright lights and glamour. For heaven's sake, Tom, it's been part of your life for the last twenty years."

"What the hell, you're worth it, Janelle. I thought you wanted me to be less selfish. It's all well lost for love."

The undercurrent of cynicism conveyed his real feelings.

"Less selfish, yes, but it's still unrealistic," she repeated, "and unrealistic sacrifices are meaningless."

"Meaning you turn that offer down, too." He turned and walked to the window.

"You're just mad because your setup didn't work." Janelle lay back on the pillows, trying to look nonchalant while tears built below the surface.

He looked over his shoulder at her, and exasperation laced his words. "What are you talking about?"

"You get us in bed, make love and then spring this new plan on me. I thought we agreed a long time ago not to play those kinds of games. If you wanted to talk about it, why didn't you bring it up before?"

"Because last time I decided to 'bring it up,' you nearly bit my head off." He left his spot by the window and stalked back to her side of the bed as he spoke. "Make up your mind, Nell. I can't seem to win, no matter what approach I use. And I'm getting damn tired of playing to your moods.

"You know, Janelle, I think you don't want to change the status quo. I think you're afraid of committing yourself, and moving in together is more of a commitment than you're willing to make."

He grabbed his shirt and walked to the door. "I'll see you later."

Janelle ignored the door that he shut a little too carefully. She made the bed and listened for the car engine as Tom sped away.

She held off the tears until she was out of the shower and about to put on her makeup. Then she sat at the vanity in the bathroom and sobbed, afraid that she would cry all night. Tom's words echoed through her tears, and she tried to confront his accusations.

What *was* the matter with her? Was she really unwilling to face commitment? Or was it that she just wasn't ready for the next step? What was wrong with taking the whole thing a little more slowly? Why did it always have to be at Tom's speed, on his terms? She couldn't just upset her life and her whole family's by announcing she was moving to Chicago.

A fresh spate of tears accompanied the realization that she was afraid to ask for what she needed. He'd been willing to make concessions without her asking before. Why couldn't she just tell him she needed more time? Of all the people in his world, surely the woman he loved was the one person who could ask for something, could tell him what she needed.

She forced herself to stop crying. He was wrong about one thing. She loved him and wanted their relationship to work.

But there was more to it than that. He brought life to her existence and the world to her doorstep. Was it so wrong that she wanted him on those terms, in her world, without becoming part of his?

She stared at herself in the mirror. Even *she* could hear the selfishness in that. But he was being just as selfish, and unrealistic as well. How could she make him see that compromise meant finding solutions that would work for both of them? Commuting to Jackson would wear both of them out in no time. But living in that pile of bricks in Chicago wouldn't work either. Even in ideal circumstances she wasn't sure she could ever adjust to the high-profile life-style.

Drying her eyes, she tried to cover the damage with makeup and hurried through the rest of her routine. The last thing she wanted was to have everyone start speculating. The thought of all that well-meaning curiosity brought her near tears again, but this time she conquered them.

The polka party was in full swing by the time she arrived. Even though children weren't allowed in the beer tent, its entry was blocked by hoards of young faces, watching and calculating the years until they could join the fun.

Janelle scanned the crowd as she approached the tent and saw Tippy and Dan turning away. She called to them and they slowed. Dan was smiling, but Tippy looked disgusted. "Don't go in there, Janelle. Dad's acting like a jerk."

Janelle smiled. She didn't really feel like smiling but made the effort anyway, waiting for the rest of the girl's comments.

Dan nudged Tippy with his arm. "Oh, come on, Tippy. Everyone looks stupid when they're learning to polka."

"Well, it didn't help any that he was in that beer-drinking contest. I mean, he's always preaching to me about being responsible. It was disgusting."

Janelle was torn between hurrying into the tent and staying awhile to listen to Tippy. She decided she'd already been selfish enough for one day and turned to walk toward the food hall with the children. Besides, she admitted to herself, she wasn't quite ready for another confrontation.

Dan had other ideas. "Mom, Tippy and I are going home to change out of these clothes. I can't stand this stupid tie another minute. Then we're going down to the river to watch the fireworks."

"What about dinner?" Janelle could see her plans to escape fading away.

"We ate already," Tippy said, lowering her head in apology. "Sorry, but we were hungry."

Accepting her sentence to the beer tent, Janelle patted the girl on the arm. "Okay, but really, you two, I want you to stay together and be very careful. Don't get too—"

"—close to the fireworks," Dan finished for her. He gave Tippy a long-suffering look. "She says that every year."

The two were off, and Janelle approached the tent as though she was heading to the dentist. The room was dense with smoke despite fans ventilating the canvas room. Spotlights lit the stage and also focused on the same polka band that played every year. In front of the band, a group of men in T-shirts sat behind a long table.

Obviously Tom had only participated in the qualifying rounds of the beer-drinking contest because the finals were now underway. With everyone's attention focused on the four men on the wooden platform, she was able to make her way inside virtually unnoticed.

Actually, there were five men on stage. Tom Wineski stood to the side with a microphone in one hand, a carefully measured pitcher of beer in the other. With elaborate care he handed the pitcher to the first competitor. Accompanied by a drumroll, Tom announced the contestant's name, then began the countdown. "On your mark...get set...Go!" he shouted into the microphone as the crowd came alive with cheers of encouragement. In less than thirty seconds, the man poured the brew down his throat. Janelle watched with fascinated disbelief. She generally avoided this competition, but couldn't resist a flash of amazement that anyone could swallow that much liquid that fast.

She turned her attention to Tom, who was taking healthy swigs of beer out of a nearby pitcher. If she could get a little closer, she could tell exactly how drunk he was and how much of his act was real. From where she stood, he presented a pretty convincing picture of a man well on his way to a hangover.

It was obvious that he wasn't watching for her. He wasn't paying attention to any of the women who crowded around the bandstand either. She made her way halfheartedly through the crowd, suspecting she was the only completely sober person in the room.

She tried to catch Tom's eye, but he was the ultimate showman and felt compelled to entertain the folks in between contestants. Janelle had to admire how quickly he reacted to the crowd's expectations. It reminded her of the public appearance in Chicago and how the teens had seen King at his most brash. At least he wasn't King with this group. But he wasn't being himself either. Tippy was right, he was acting like a jerk.

Janelle knew Tom saw her, yet he continued to treat her as one of the crowd. No special look, no wave, nothing more than the same polished smile he gave everyone. A start of surprise ignited a spark of anger, and she warmed to the feeling. Why, the jerk thinks he's going to give me a taste of life without him!

The din rose and the crowd surged forward. Tom finally looked directly at her through narrowed eyes, apparently understanding every word she thought. She stared back, communicating without a sound. If that's the way you want it, it's fine with me, buster! Life will be a lot simpler without you.

As the crowd applauded the winner, Janelle worked her way back through the throng. She could hear Tom presenting the trophy to the champion drinker. As she edged her way out of the tent, he called for the polka band to swing into action.

Ten

Janelle took a deep breath and pulled open the screen door. She could distinguish her mother-in-law's voice, and recognized Ned's shout at his son. The Harpers were gathering for Sunday dinner. Tom and Tippy were supposed to be there as well. She hadn't seen Tom's car in the driveway, but supposed he'd come with Kathy and Ned.

She stood on the front porch a few moments, trying to organize her thoughts. She hadn't yet resolved her feelings of the night before and was loath to let the whole family in on such a personal argument. She wondered what the others would say once they sensed the tension.

As she stepped into the room, Elvin came forward to give her a hug. "Nell, we were wondering when you were going to get here."

As she returned her father-in-law's hearty embrace, she scanned the room over his shoulder. Tom hadn't arrived yet. Inevitably, she was caught in a round of welcomes, and Kathy told her what she wanted to know.

"I tell you, Nell, Tom has one sore head today. He must have partied all night. He got back to our place about three. I woke him up when we left, but I'm not sure what kind of shape he's in." Kathy watched Janelle expectantly, obviously hoping for some explanation of why Janelle hadn't been with him last night.

Janelle tried to make light of the news. "When I left the beer tent it looked like he was ready to polka with just about anyone."

"Janelle, dear, I'm glad you're here." Irene Harper stood in the kitchen doorway. "Could you come in the kitchen a minute. I want you to give me the list of ingredients for that new potato-salad recipe."

Grateful for a place to hide, Janelle stayed in the kitchen most of the afternoon, gently turning aside any questions about Tom's whereabouts with the suggestion that they "get the story from Kathy."

About three o'clock, just before everyone sat down to eat, she heard the familiar purr of the Porsche and knew Tom had finally arrived. She didn't go out to greet him but stayed in the kitchen, letting her anger simmer along with the vegetables on the stove. The root of the anger—compromise and the lack of it—was pushed to the back of her mind. It was his behavior that rankled now.

Before long the meal was ready, the tables set out back, the children served. Irene took off her apron and headed for the back door. "Janelle, would you go in there and shoo them all outside before the kids finish everything."

Once more Janelle stood at the door and took a deep breath before walking in. Tom seemed to feel her presence immediately. He was sitting on the back of the sofa wearing a hangover and a day-old growth of beard. She watched him break off his conversation with Ned and turn to face her. Despite the strain around his eyes and the dark shadow on his chin, Janelle's heart lurched into its double-time tattoo. She tried to tell herself it was anger, but anger never generated the heartfelt longing that was pulsing through her.

She waited at the door and he smiled. It was a half smile, not of happiness, but an apology of sorts. He raised his eyebrows and his smile slipped, replaced by an arrogant demand for acceptance.

Janelle shook her head in exasperation rather than denial and called the group in general to dinner, avoiding further eye contact with Tom. Without another word she turned back to the kitchen and picked up the last platter of bratwurst to bring to the picnic table.

So the argument had become an impasse. The sense of loss forced her to bite her lip to keep the tears from falling. For just a moment she hated him for his arrogance, for his take-me-as-I-am mentality.

The residue of that feeling kept her silent and distant for the rest of the afternoon. Did she really want one more chance to say all the wrong things? Tom kept his distance, too, seeming to sense that conversation now would only increase the growing breach between them.

Tom was first to leave, despite the fact that Tippy kept pressing to "stay a little longer." It was Irene who reminded the girl that her dad had been dancing all night.

"You be sure to talk to him all the way home, just to keep him awake."

As usual, all the Harpers gathered on the porch for goodbyes. Janelle walked halfway down the path to the car, but stopped short of the driveway and murmured a conventional farewell. Tom turned and stared at her a moment, a muscle twitching in his cheek. With Tippy a few steps ahead, they finally had their moment alone together and Janelle stood silent, unsure what to say, unsure how she felt. She watched Tippy load her gear into the Porsche and waited.

Tom didn't say anything, either, then moved through the gate and snapped it shut. The gesture drew Janelle's eyes away from Tippy. Once he had her full attention, he seemed to lose interest in it and turned to walk down the drive.

"I'll call you sometime." He tossed the line over his shoulder, and Janelle nodded to his retreating back.

* * *

Rain pounded down on the tin roof covering the porch. Rivers of water overflowed the gutters, digging soggy trenches in the remnants of the fall flowers that lined the back wall. Janelle told herself the rain was the reason for her depression. She tried to convince herself that this was the first weekend all summer and fall that it had rained and that the endless drip and spatter had her on edge. It wasn't because she hadn't heard from Tom. It wasn't because he hadn't shown up on her doorstep Friday night, just in time for a root-beer float.

Janelle pulled a basket of apples from the refrigerator, planning on making a big batch of applesauce. She sat at the kitchen table peeling a long slice of red as she worked her way through the first falls from the backyard tree. It was a routine almost as comforting as working in the garden, and Janelle's actions were automatic. As she cut and peeled, her thoughts drifted, trying once again to come to terms with the end of her relationship with Tom.

It's over, she thought. Why couldn't she just accept that it was over? Janelle had been chanting the phrase for days, and still she couldn't quite believe that she would never see him again. She buried that notion under layers of other feelings, especially the residue of a week-long grudge.

She couldn't remember the last time she had nursed resentment for so long. Maybe it was because they hadn't resolved anything. She'd had a whole week to ponder every detail, including that arrogant half smile she was sure he'd meant as an apology.

Sitting in her kitchen now, she had to admit that his confidence was also one of the things she loved about him. How could it be that you could love and hate the very same qualities? Had it been that way with Arnie? If it had, she'd forgotten.

Confidence, arrogance—both the terms and how she felt about them were moot now. She would never have to learn how to deal with either.

Maybe the grudge lingered because she hadn't talked to anyone about their argument. There wasn't anyone she wanted to talk to but Tom, and he hadn't even given her the chance. There hadn't been a call from Chicago for ten days.

His parting promise to call her sometime had gone unfulfilled. Sometime was stretching into never, and Janelle was trying to figure out how to cope with it. The fall garden was already in better shape than it had ever been, but her usual coping mechanism was failing her. Now she was working on the apples, hoping the welcome routine would help her get over the sense of loss she remembered too well.

That sense of loss was one more layer of heartache. At least Arnie's death had been final. This loneliness, mixed with the faint hope Tom would call, was a torture all its own. He was still so close. Only as far away as the television, as close as a celebrity magazine, as easy to reach as the telephone. More than once she'd considered calling, and each time had to remind herself of that long-ago promise never to ask for more than he was willing to give. But she'd pondered the situation over and over again during those long sleepless nights. Of all the people in his world, who were more important to Tom than the people he loved? Didn't people who love each other have the right to ask for what they needed? And wasn't it unrealistic to expect him to be a mind reader? Even conceding the truth in these questions, she was still unwilling to make a phone call that could mean rejection and pain.

She put the apples on to cook and pulled the canning jars off the shelf. She plunked them on the stove and pulled out a couple of lids, welcoming the clatter she was creating.

At the bottom of her jumbled feelings was an inability to decide if there was any truth to Tom's accusation that she was a coward. Was it the fear of loving and losing again that had held her back? Or was she really motivated by making sure her needs had equal billing with his? Either way, she sounded just as selfish as he did. Maybe they were both incapable of reaching for what they needed. Maybe their notions of a future together had been illusory.

Putting thoughts of Tom from her mind, she concentrated on the applesauce in front of her. But she couldn't keep from wondering if it was raining in Chicago.

"You sure you want to make this move, Tom?" Harris leaned back in his chair and tapped his pen on the desk. "It's a big change. I thought between us, Nelson and I had come up with a pretty good proposal. He's a damn good agent. You're paying him a lot for his advice."

Tom stood up, ran a hand through his hair and paced the room. "Listen, Harris, it's not like I'm asking out of the show. They'll have me every episode if they want." He shrugged his shoulders. "So, the idea's a little different. One of the things I pay you both for is to sell my ideas to the bigwigs. Besides, you know Casey Stanton is good. They ought to develop her role more."

Harris held up his hand. "I'm not telling them how to run the show, Tom. The story line is not our territory, unless you want Nelson to work that into the contract, too?"

Tom shook his head, unfazed by his manager's sarcasm. "I don't much care what they do. I've got other things on my mind."

"I know, I know." Harris snapped the folder shut and buzzed for his secretary.

Tom took the cue; their meeting was over. The secretary entered and Tom stood to leave. "Thanks for everything, Harris. I'm glad we got the contract squared away. I'll see you in L.A."

Tom grabbed his raincoat from the couch in the front office and had it buttoned and belted before he stepped out the front door. He was glad the limousine was only a few feet away as a gust of wind threw a bucket of rain against him. It was a short ride to the airport and he sat back, for once grateful that someone else was doing the driving.

With weather like this, the plane would be delayed. Maybe he would have time to call Tippy. He checked his watch and realized that she wouldn't be home from school yet.

He could call Janelle. The thought tiptoed around the corner of his subconscious. For the first time in a week Tom didn't bat it away, but gave the idea careful consideration.

The VIP lounge would have a quiet spot with a phone.

She would probably be home.

He was desperately lonely without her.

But what would he say? What could he say that he hadn't said already. *I love you. I want to be with you. Not just every now and then, but forever.* He'd said all that before, and it hadn't worked any magic. He'd offered to give it all up for her, and she still refused. Now what could he say? *Come with me to Los Angeles for two weeks. Hang around while I work eighteen-hour days.* God help her, if she didn't like the Chicago life-style, she would last less than a day in Tinseltown.

He decided to cancel the phone call. It would be better to wait until he was back home with enough time to see her in person, anyway.

Unrealistic sacrifice is meaningless. The stupid phrase had haunted him for days until he admitted the truth of it. She was right. Some of his ideas had been just for show. But that wasn't any reason to dump the whole relationship.

He assured himself it was just a temporary setback, and he was beginning to believe it. If he had his way, it would be just the first of a lifetime's worth. He smiled to himself. Hopefully, they would figure out a quicker way to resolve them in the future. This kind of long-term, long-distance anger wasn't good at all.

It had taken distance and some lonely nights before he was willing to accept that Janelle wasn't as ready to deepen the relationship as he was. The first hint had been in Chicago. She told him she wasn't ready, and he hadn't been listening. Then he pushed it with the confrontation in Jackson, and the realization had hit him straight on.

At first his ego had suffered—hence his behavior at the polka party. It massaged his wounded pride and proved to himself and to her that he was important to someone, even if it was to an anonymous crowd. He'd proved it all right, and she'd told him without words exactly how impressed she was. He hadn't known what to say or do the next day, and his promise to call had sounded lame even to his own ears.

Once he was home it hadn't taken long to sort through his own feelings and comprehend hers. Now he realized that he'd always been the one to push for the next step. If that was the pattern of their relationship, then so be it. He would just keep pushing, but maybe with a little more finesse. He'd watched Harris for years—it was about time he learned a little something from the way the guy handled people. Janelle called it manipulating. Maybe it was. But one thing he'd learned lately; there was a right way and a wrong way to do it.

He'd thought about calling every day since, debated sending flowers, flying or driving up to see her. He hadn't done any of them and wondered at his reason for silence. He shifted uncomfortably in the seat. Maybe he was afraid of what she would say. Maybe he was afraid that she'd had enough and it was over. Maybe she didn't love him anymore.

Janelle was the first person in years, maybe in his whole adult life that he'd been willing to open himself up to. She was the first woman to know him without pretense, and he hadn't been good enough. Stripped of his confidence, Tom Wineski winced at the feelings of inadequacy that seeped through him. The sensation only lasted a moment.

He'd spent his life beating the odds, he reminded himself, and he wasn't going to stop now.

Tom glanced around the elegant hotel dining room and counted five familiar faces. A couple nodded back and one smiled. The others were too engrossed in their own conversations to pay him any attention.

He watched Harris as he worked his way through the room. At the rate he was stopping to chat, Tom would be late for his flight. He'd wondered why Harris had suggested breakfast together, anyway. They'd tied up all the loose ends last night, and he could have been on the first plane home. He understood as he watched Harris laugh and slap someone on the back. This was a chance to see and be seen.

"Morning, Tom." Harris pulled out the chair and sat down as the waiter hurried over to pour him some coffee and take his order. Harris seemed tired, but as in control as ever.

He handed Tom a packet of papers. "Sorry I forgot to give you these last night. All the partying out here is enough to distract anyone."

Tom laughed. "Yeah, I noticed exactly how distracted you were. No wonder you look so tired this morning."

"Always on the lookout for new clients." His tone of voice changed, and a little smile teased his mouth. "I've got news, Tom."

Caught by his confidential tone, Tom turned his full attention to his manager.

"You made the right move, buddy. Word of your contract change has gotten around. Sinjin approached me last night about a feature-length movie based on that cameo bit you played earlier in the year." Tom leaned forward, listening intently. "Apparently they've just finished the editing, and you're the best thing about a pretty predictable movie. You know how sequels are really big right now, so they decided they might like to try a variation on that and develop a story line around your character."

Tom knew he should be excited. Harris obviously thought that was what he'd had in mind when he'd suggested contract changes in the first place. His exact words had been that he wanted more time to pursue other interests—he couldn't blame Harris for interpreting that as meaning movie work.

It wasn't what he meant at all. He'd been thinking about Janelle and the time they needed to build a relationship, a marriage.

"The idea sounds feasible, Harris. But it's not what I want right now." Tom sat back and waited for the inevitable question.

Harris leaned forward, the smile gone, his face a bland mask that didn't even hint at what he was thinking. "Then how about explaining to me exactly what you do have in mind. It's a little hard to represent you without your overall game plan."

"Marriage," he said, quickly looking around the room to see if anyone had overheard. Everyone was absorbed in their own conversations—but the statement did, however, garner Harris's full attention.

The man looked flabbergasted. For once the cool exterior was gone. "What the hell are you talking about Tom?"

"Listen, the only reason I'm telling you this is because you have a right to know. As you said, you need the game plan. And that's it in one word. Right now the lady isn't even speaking to me. I'm hoping to change that soon and then, with any luck at all, there'll be wedding bells."

"That's what you had in mind when you pulled those last-minute changes in the contract talks?"

"Yup."

Harris looked totally puzzled for a moment, then he smiled. "Janelle Harper, that sweet little thing you brought to the mall appearance." The smile grew. "The mall appearance you tried to cancel."

Tom tried to look neutral, but he couldn't stop smiling.

Harris continued to speculate. "She doesn't like sharing you with the public, and so you're trying to make peace with a few strategic changes."

"That's not it exactly, Harris, but near enough. We both need to compromise a little. What we've got is worth keeping."

"Sure, sure, I hear that all the time. My sister's been in and out of love five times and every time it's something worth keeping. Only problem is, she never does. Hope it's not going to be the same with you."

Tom shook his head slowly and with conviction.

"Okay, I get the message. Janelle Harper is the 'other interest,' and I should keep the rest on hold."

"Right. Don't get me wrong—I want a career, and movies sound like the way to go, but from now on it's a joint decision." He glanced at his watch and got up. "Now, if I don't hustle I'm going to miss my flight. You'll be back in Chicago on Friday?" Harris nodded. "Good. I'll see you next week sometime."

Janelle ran up the basement steps two at a time. She grabbed the phone in midring and took a breath. "Harpers'."

All she heard were sniffles and the slight static of a long-distance connection. "Janelle?" The voice was wavery and hesitant, and Janelle recognized it right away.

"Tippy? Tippy, honey, what's the matter?"

"Janelle, I really need help. I can't find my Dad...." The words stopped as more muffled sobs echoed through the line.

"Tippy, I can help you, but you have to calm down and tell me what's the matter." Janelle gripped the phone as though her grasp would convey security and scrambled for the pad and pencil on the nearby counter. She tried to make her voice sound firm and authoritative. "First, where is your father?" Please God, she thought, let Tom be all right.

"He's in California on business. I tried to call him at his hotel, but they said he'd already checked out. He might be on the plane, but no one in Harris's office knows for sure when he's coming home."

"Why do you need your Dad? Are you supposed to be staying with him."

"Not really." The tears started again. "But last night, Cliff, you know my Mom's boyfriend, he made a pass at me and I got scared...."

Janelle tried to tell herself to be calm, not to get upset. Tippy was upset enough already. Her voice was curt with the effort. "Where are you now?"

"I came to my Dad's. It was the only place I could think
of, and I had a key. Please don't be mad at me, Janelle. I
really didn't do anything."

"Honey, I'm not one bit mad at you. It's that horrible
Cliff I'm mad at."

"Janelle, could you come stay with me until Dad comes
home?"

"Sure I can, but it'll take me a couple of hours to get
there. Will you be okay? I could call my sister and have her
come stay with you until I get there."

"No, I think I'll be okay. All the doors are locked, and I
can hide in my room until you come. I called school and
pretended I was Mom. They think I'm sick."

The ride seemed interminable. The route was familiar and
she was making good time, but somehow the minutes ticked
by with excruciating slowness and sixty miles an hour felt
like a snail's pace.

Maybe she should have tried to call Harris before she left.
But she didn't even know if that was his first or last name.
She'd debated calling Elaine but decided that would violate
Tippy's confidence. For some reason the child had been
unwilling to talk to her mother. Maybe she would get a few
more answers when she got to Tom's house.

Where was Tom, anyway? Tippy said in California. Why
hadn't he called and asked for help with Tippy? Okay, she
knew the answer to that, but she would have been willing to
help out. Just because she'd been mad at Tom didn't mean
she would vent that anger on a young girl as vulnerable as
Tippy.

As she pulled into the driveway of Tom's house, the front
door flew open and Tippy ran down the steps to throw herself into Janelle's arms. "Oh, I'm so glad you're here, Janelle."

"Me, too. We've really missed you."

"Yeah, so have I. Dad's been real quiet or real grumpy,
and I can't decide which is worse. I guess he misses you, too.

When I talked to him two days ago, he promised a trip to Jackson as soon as he got back.''

That was news to Janelle, good news. Despite the concern over Tippy, Janelle couldn't repress the surge of hopefulness replacing the misery that had dogged her waking hours and made a mockery of sleep.

She hugged the girl close one more time and led her inside.

Twenty minutes later Janelle was on the phone, pumping Harris's secretary for information on Tom's return. With a clear picture of the situation, she decided that Tom would be home before dark and that Elaine was too engrossed in her new career in real estate to pay much attention to whether Tippy came home from school on time or not.

Tippy had suggested that she just call and tell her Mom that she was with a friend. Janelle was impressed with the maneuverings of the teenage mind, but suggested they save that ploy for later.

They were sitting in the kitchen, cleaning up after a late lunch. A quick trip to the local grocery store had restocked the refrigerator, and Janelle had finished an apple cake for dessert and was in the midst of making a meat loaf for dinner. She didn't want Tom to think she was taking over, but thought it was important to surround Tippy with an air of normalcy. Janelle felt trapped between the need to help Tippy through an obviously traumatic experience and the frustration she felt at being forced to meet Tom without any overture on his part. She hoped he wouldn't think that she'd come down here desperate for a reconciliation.

Her own feelings aside, Janelle realized that Tippy needed her and considered a way to broach the incident that had precipitated the emergency. She'd thought about leaving it for Tom, but he was bound to be furious and it wouldn't hurt if she had a head start.

"Tippy." The girl looked up from the teen magazine that had just arrived in the mail. "I was hoping you would tell me what happened with Cliff."

"I really don't want to talk about it at all, Janelle. It was so embarrassing." She wouldn't look Janelle in the eye and started flipping through the pages of the magazine absently.

"I won't press you, but you know you're going to have to explain it to your Dad. I thought maybe it would help if you talked to me first."

Tears filled Tippy's eyes, and Janelle wiped her hands on a paper towel before walking over to sit next to her. "I just don't want my dad to be mad at me. He's always telling me I act too grown-up, and I'm afraid he'll think I was flirting or something, and I wasn't, really I wasn't."

It took a while to get the complete story out of Tippy. Her Mom had been out showing property late in the evening, and Cliff had been drinking pretty heavily. He came into the family room where Tippy was watching TV and put his arm around her, tossing out a couple of suggestive lines. Tippy had run up to her room and locked the door. And that had been it.

"Why didn't you tell your Mother?"

Tippy shrugged. "I would have, but she got home late and then was in a hurry in the morning because she had a breakfast meeting. Cliff was still asleep, and I wanted to get out of there before he got up."

It sounded pretty sensible to Janelle. "Your Dad should be here sometime soon. So I guess we can wait and let him talk to your Mom. In the meantime, let me finish this meat loaf, and then we can find something else to do.

"How about if we repot the spider plants." Tippy pointed to the plants hanging in the kitchen eating area.

"They do look like they're about to expire from overcrowding." Once again she worried about Tom's reaction to all this domesticity, but keeping Tippy occupied won out over her desire to appear disinterested. "Do you have the potting soil and pots?"

"Yeah, Dad and I got them a couple of weeks ago. He said you'd have a fit if you saw them like that."

A couple of weeks ago. Janelle could hardly remember that long ago, before those heated, useless words, back when life seemed perfect.

"Janelle? Could we listen to the radio while we work?"

"Sure, on the condition that you go haul all the things we need in here."

Tippy jumped off the stool in a flash and hurried out the back door.

Janelle shook her head at the sudden mood swing and smiled at the resilience of young people. Patting the meat loaf into shape, she put it in a small roasting pan and set it on the stove until Tom came home.

As uncomfortable as she felt in the oversized house, as worried as she was about Tom's reaction to her presence, there was a certain appeal about waiting for Tom, with his daughter nearby and dinner in the oven. Maybe what she really needed was to see him again to get her priorities in order.

She told herself that was a fantasy. If he wanted someone to cook his dinner he could hire a housekeeper. She'd come to help Tippy and told herself not to confuse that with a lifetime of caring that Tom might not want.

With the last of the utensils air-drying on the drain board, she wiped her hands and considered going out to help Tippy. Then she heard the front door open and a familiar voice. Tom was back.

Eleven

Nell! Hey, Janelle!'' Tom looked for some sign of Janelle in the entrance hall. There was none. In fact, the house seemed empty. But her blue sedan was in the driveway. Tom threw his bag and coat on a chair and headed for the kitchen. He didn't know whether to be pleased or wary, but either way, he couldn't repress the surge of happiness that obliterated days of melancholy. He pushed through the swinging door to find Janelle leaning against the sink. His smile faded. It wasn't welcome he read in those eyes. It was the same wariness he felt. But why was she here, if she wasn't anxious to see him?

Maybe if he'd acted on the impulse to send flowers or call, she would be smiling at him. Instead, she was watching him as though he were some sort of unwelcome guest. Hell, this was his house.

The back door flew open and Tippy staggered in, laden with potting soil and clay pots. When she saw Tom, her face showed anxiety and a little panic. "Oh, Dad, you're home."

"Yeah, I was kind of hoping for a warmer reception. How about a hug." Then it registered that something was out of kilter. It was more than Janelle's unexpected presence. Tippy's expression, maybe. Then the incongruity struck him. "Hey, what are you doing here, Tippy?"

He held Tippy at arm's length, holding on to her hands. He tried to prompt her. "Did you have a problem with your mother?" Tom glanced at Janelle, who nodded at Tippy.

Tippy pulled her hands out of Tom's and moved closer to Janelle. "It wasn't Mom, Dad. It was Cliff. He, umm, he uhh..."

Janelle put her arm around Tippy. Her expression had softened, but it seemed to Tom that she was trying to protect the child.

"Tom, Cliff made things a little uncomfortable for Tippy. He was drinking a lot and Elaine wasn't home. Cliff made some suggestive remarks, and Tippy very wisely decided that it would be better to come back here and wait for you. She called me and asked if I'd come and stay with her."

Shoot him for being a lousy father, but Tom's first thought was that Janelle hadn't come of her own accord. She was there because Tippy needed someone and he hadn't been available. He was angry at himself for failing as a father, and he was unreasonably angry at Janelle for being there when he wasn't. Then the implications of Janelle's story hit him. Most of all he was furious with Cliff. "That bastard! Wait till I get my hands on him."

He looked at Janelle and read a plea for understanding rather than temper. He turned to Tippy and tried to cool down. He wasn't an actor for nothing. He checked his anger and spoke as calmly as he could. "You were smart, Tippy. You did the right thing, honey."

He paused, parental fear overriding his actor's persona. "You're telling the truth, aren't you? All he did was talk? You know nothing that happened would ever affect how much we love you."

"Oh, Dad, you sound like one of those after-school specials." Tippy took a deep breath and the cynicism disappeared. "Nothing happened. He just scared me, and he's always been such a complete jerk." Now she looked impish. "Besides, I hadn't seen Janelle in a long time and thought it would be a nice surprise if she was here when you got home."

The two adults glanced at each other and then back at Tippy. Noting her smile, Tom's flare of anger faded. Before it completely evaporated, he decided he'd better call Elaine and get a few things straight.

"Listen, I'm going in the office to call your mother. I think she and I need to have a little talk." He pointed to the pile of gardening debris by the back door. "What's that mess?"

Janelle followed his gaze. "We were going to repot the spider plants hanging by the bay window."

Tom nodded. "Great, why don't you do that while I call Elaine."

Gardening of any sort was new to Tippy. As they worked their way through the process, it held her complete attention, and she didn't seem the slightest bit inclined to eavesdrop on her dad's conversation.

Working with the rich potting soil, Janelle thought of all the implications of the work she and Tippy were doing. People had to grow and change, too. After all, if they didn't, life would get awfully boring. Is that what had happened to her complacent, content existence? Had Tom been responsible for just enough growth and change that the small town no longer suited her needs?

"That was absolutely amazing."

Janelle jumped as Tom walked in, preoccupied and thoughtful.

"What is?"

"Elaine." He shook his head, not looking at Janelle but addressing the room in general. "Elaine and I actually had a civil conversation. Even more amazing, we agreed on something."

"And what did you agree about?" Janelle couldn't stop a small smile. He looked so perplexed, like a kid whose mom had praised a bad report card.

"She's going to kick Cliff out. Today, she said." He finally came out of his reverie and stared directly at Janelle. "You should have heard her, Nell. She was furious. It made my reaction look calm." He paused for a moment. "Of course, it could be there's a little ego involved."

More than a little, Janelle thought, remembering the woman she'd seen at the courthouse, struggling to hold back the years. "I'm glad you resolved that so easily. It would have been awful if she refused to believe Tippy."

Tom ran a hand through his hair and nodded. "Yeah, it's what I was afraid would happen." He looked at Janelle, his expression uncertain. "Do you think I should make an issue of this, press charges or something? Those damn tabloids would be bound to get hold of it." He winced at the thought.

Janelle walked closer and faced him, the kitchen counter separating them. "I think it would do more harm than good, at least as far as Tippy's concerned. Since Cliff won't be an issue anymore, my inclination would be to let it go."

Tom nodded.

There was a moment of silence as the two of them stared at each other. Janelle wanted to reach out and to run at the same time. She waited for some sign, not even sure what kind of sign she hoped for.

"Now that we've put out all the fires, you and I need to talk." Tom reached across the counter and put his hand over hers.

The gesture didn't do much to soften the arrogance of his statement. Was the man ever going to learn? Janelle pulled her hand away and immediately regretted the reflex action. The moment of communication was gone.

"You're being a coward, Janelle. What we have is too good to give up."

"A coward? This from a man who had two weeks to call and couldn't bring himself to pick up the phone?"

"I had reasons for that. Listen, there were some major contract negotiations going on...."

Janelle's sigh wasn't an act. She was tired of the story.

She walked around the counter, deliberately cutting a wide path to avoid Tom. She took off her apron and dropped it on one of the stools. "I have to go. Katherine's expecting me for dinner."

"It smells like you've got dinner cooking here."

"That was just to keep Tippy busy until you got back. You can eat it or throw it out. It's meat loaf."

"And apple cake?" Tom guessed with an exaggerated sniff that brought the fragrance of cinnamon and apple.

Janelle nodded. "Really, Tom, I have to leave before traffic gets bad."

Tom didn't stop smiling and moved so she could pass. "All right, all right. But before you go, there's just one thing I want to remind you of."

She turned to face him, her back to the swinging door. "Yes."

He smiled and took his time, folding his hands across his chest and nodding as he spoke. "I love you and I'm not going to give up until we're back together."

By all rights she should have had a miserable night's sleep. A strange bed was always difficult to get used to, and that was the least of what was on her mind. There was so much unsettled between them. And despite, or maybe because of, Tom's last statement, sleep should have been restless.

Janelle slept soundly. She woke to the memory of Tom's declaration and the very platonic goodbye that had followed. She awoke to an overwhelming feeling of well-being that had nothing to do with the comfortable surroundings of her sister's home.

Katherine had questioned her mood last night. "You know, Janelle, you just haven't been yourself these last two weeks. You're definitely not the brooding type." Katherine had turned to her husband. "Do you think it's love?"

It was a rhetorical question, and she turned back to her sister. "Janelle, just remember. You won't get anywhere unless you two talk about it. You always want to be so self-sufficient. You'll do anything for anyone but never ask for anything yourself. It used to drive me nuts when we were kids. You'd cry then and wouldn't tell me what was wrong."

Janelle shrugged her shoulders, still not inclined to speak.

"You don't have to tell me a thing. Tom's the one you have to talk to. Don't shut the guy out. Give him a chance."

That drew a response. "You know, Katherine, people are always making demands on him. It was one thing I never thought I'd do. Besides, he can be so darned arrogant. Not so much as a please or thank-you."

"Janelle. Sometimes coming on strong is the only way to push you into action. You *do* have a tendency to be stubborn."

Janelle smiled as she remembered how she'd bristled at her sister's criticism. The fact was, Katherine was right. She thought back over Tom's actions and his words. He'd tried to convince her that they had a future, and she'd ignored the signs until he'd come on so strong that she'd rejected him out of hand as arrogant.

Maybe if she mellowed a little, he would drop the pushy facade and revert to the man who'd won her love.

Humming along with the radio, Janelle showered, then she invaded Katherine's closet for exactly the right thing to wear. She settled on a two-piece knit dress in a lovely sky blue that Tom would insist matched her eyes. She stepped close to the mirror and stared at herself. Her eyes were as hazel as ever, but if Tom was telling the truth and not color-blind, they would be turning blue soon enough.

She steeled herself to call Tom to see if he was free. She walked into the kitchen to find a note tacked to the bulletin board. "Tom called. Will be here at noon."

She poured herself a cup of coffee and considered the note. You could read it as arrogant, she thought, or it could be he was giving her an easy way out. All she had to do was get in her car and drive away before the doorbell rang.

Instead, she stayed at the kitchen table, half listening to the radio and toying with a second cup of coffee. The doughnuts were tempting, but she could barely swallow a bite. A combination of nerves and excitement robbed her of her appetite.

She took the coffee service and carried it to the living room. Standing by the window, she watched the waves of Lake Michigan pound the shore and tried to marshal her thoughts. Tom was due any minute, and she wasn't at all sure what to say.

At the moment all she wanted to do was tell him how much she loved him. Worries about his life-style and hers seemed inconsequential. How could she even think that after having endangered the whole relationship because of it? Maybe it was all part of the process. Maybe they needed the time to put it all into perspective, to realize that solutions could be found, once the problems were confronted.

The buzzer sounded, announcing Tom's arrival. She walked slowly down the hall, rehearsing a dozen greetings, and opened the door just as he buzzed again. She caught a look of panic on his face, as though he thought maybe she'd left. A sigh of relief followed and the beginnings of a smile that faded almost as fast.

"You're still here?"

It wasn't exactly a question. Janelle read every nuance of tone and body, the way he stood uncertainly on the threshold, his body turned slightly as if to protect himself from a possible blow. It was Tom at his most vulnerable. Tom with all his arrogance gone, Tom Wineski looking, almost begging, for something he'd found and almost lost. It sliced through her mind that she was the only one who would ever see him like this. She was the only one capable of stripping away the arrogance. Because she was the one he loved, she had the power to hurt and heal.

"I'm still here." She nodded, her growing smile mirroring his. "And not going anywhere soon."

Without another word he swept her into his arms. His lips caught hers in a kiss that erased pain and replaced it with longing. For a moment she let him control, reveling in the way his mouth crushed hers. Then she opened her lips and welcomed his more intimate kiss, her arms twined around his neck, her hands lost in the hair that threaded through her fingers as she pressed him closer. Every word he hadn't said, every flower he hadn't sent, every call he hadn't made was forgotten in that simple intimate exchange of love.

He eased his hold and then swept her into a fierce hug that was as possessive as it was passionate.

"There were times when I never thought I'd see those blue eyes again." He smiled and she smiled back.

"I love you." She spoke the words with conviction, giving voice to the feelings vibrating around them.

He pulled her back into his arms and held tight. "That's all that matters. That's all that matters, sweetheart."

She couldn't let him go. But then it seemed he was of the same mind. Arm in arm they walked to the living room. She poured him some coffee, then settled on the love seat next to him. He pulled her close, and for a few moments they enjoyed the rapport, talking trivialities, her garden at home, the famous faces he'd seen in L.A.

"I do have some big news."

Janelle turned her head so she could see Tom's face. He was smiling and she nodded.

"I met with Elaine this morning. This is incredible, but she's decided to let me have custody of Tippy."

Janelle sat up straight and looked back at Tom, who was shaking his head, still surprised by the turn of events.

"Really? You're serious?"

"Absolutely. The meeting was at Katherine's office and Elaine's lawyer was there."

"Why the change of heart?" Janelle was skeptical. "Did it have something to do with Cliff?"

"That may have been a catalyst, but she said that she was working hard trying to establish herself in real estate, and that meant evenings and weekends. Basically she was willing to admit that she couldn't give Tippy the kind of attention she needs now and thought I could."

"Tom, that's fabulous. You must be thrilled." She sat facing him and he pulled her into his arms. The intense emotion of their greeting had mellowed. Now the passion grew.

"I think this is going to be a fabulous day all around. I think we're due, don't you?"

"I couldn't agree with you more. I know there are still a hundred questions to be answered and explanations to be made, but somehow just being with you is everything I need right now. Everything else will come in time."

Tom nodded.

Conversation dwindled, and Janelle lay back and smiled into Tom's eyes. "I suppose I should wash those cups." She made a halfhearted move to sit up.

Tom pulled her back against him. "Sometimes, sweetheart, you're just too sensible."

She turned in his arms. "It was just a thought." She kissed the spot right at the corner of his mouth and let her lips rest there, enjoying the erotic feel of his mouth as he spoke.

"I have a better idea."

He began to unbutton her blouse. He only undid the top two buttons and then slid his hand around her neck. Using a gentle pressure, he angled her into the corner of the love seat and pressed his thumb against her jaw to align her mouth with his. His tongue coaxed her with a gentle invasion of her mouth. His hands urged her closer. There was no rejection, no hesitation. With that kiss all restraint disappeared.

Janelle welcomed his weight as he pressed her into the soft cushions at her back. Her need equaled his. He opened the last few buttons while he teased her lips with a sweet hot caress that left her restless for more. She lay curled by his side, cradled against his body, her lips touching the base of his throat, his jawline, his cheek.

"You know, I didn't make my bed this morning," she whispered.

Tom moved up off the couch in a single motion, pulling Janelle with him. "Oh, Nell, sometimes I really admire that sensible streak."

She laughed breathlessly as he slipped her blouse off and let it flutter to the floor. Then he turned and moved down the hall. Janelle stepped out of her shoes and followed. Tom's joined hers on the hall floor. His pants fell on her skirt. By the time they reached the guest room, they'd left a trail of clothes and no doubt about their intent.

Tom pulled her down on the bed with quick impatience, as if the bare minute's separation had pushed his control to its limit. Janelle surrendered her last coherent thought to the inevitable sensual magnet, giving herself up to the arousing pleasure of his hands, his mouth and his body. As he stroked her breasts with his fingertips, he teased first one taut, sweet nipple then the other with his tongue until Janelle began to move with instinctive demand. He entwined his legs with hers, holding her trapped, yet a willing participant in the slow, intimate inspection they exchanged.

His mouth followed his look, kissing her lips, her neck, then capturing every pleasure point until her body arched and her hands pressed his body into deeper contact.

He rolled on his side, pulling her on top of him, and she immediately slid down a little, fitting herself to him. Janelle's world was a haze of feeling, bursts of pleasure so intense that she cried out a little, then buried her face in his neck as he began to move inside her.

It took too long, yet came too fast; a wealth of feeling, a rainbow of sensations encompassing the complete sharing of mutual fulfillment. He watched her with eyes wide and hazed with pleasure as his body edged them closer to the timeless sharing of their love. Janelle lay still, wanting to move, yet too full of erotic feeling to do more than savor her pleasure and his response.

Tom whispered her name once, twice, and held her close, his body suddenly tensed and still except for the throbbing stab of pleasure inside her. Janelle responded with a kiss, not moving, treasuring the intensity and welcoming the promise.

They lay still, intimately joined for a few moments. "Janelle, that was the most incredible experience I've ever had." Tom took a deep breath and smoothed her hair. "It's like the way I feel about you. Uncontrollably, madly in love and desperate to make you mine."

The edge of insecurity moved her. Tears gathered in regret for all the times she'd pushed him away, insensitive to his needs, his longing for acceptance. "I'm yours," she whispered as he kissed the tears away.

Janelle snuggled closer to his side, within the protective circle of his arm. "Nell, darling, I'm sure glad you hadn't made the bed."

Janelle's giggle was infectious. "Somehow, I don't think that would have stopped us."

He pulled her hand and urged her off the bed. "Come on, honey. If we stay here five minutes longer we'll be here all day." He looked at her, trying to suppress a laugh. "What's wrong with that, you say?"

Janelle nodded, waiting for the answer as Tom handed her her bra and slip along with a quick kiss. "Not a damn thing, but now I'm trying to be sensible, and we both know we have to talk details."

Dressing led them back to the living room, and Tom gathered up the folder and newspaper he'd brought along. "How about some breakfast first?"

Janelle nodded, suddenly finding an appetite that had vanished weeks ago.

"Great. Then we've got some house hunting to do."

They were in Tom's car, heading toward an unfamiliar part of suburban Chicago. Tom turned off the main road onto a quiet residential street. "I told Harris exactly what I thought you'd like, and he came up with three places. I checked them out after my meeting with Elaine, and I think this one's it." He was checking the map, maneuvering the car and talking at the same time.

Janelle was more worried about arriving in one piece than anything else. "No more talking. Just concentrate on getting us there. I'm going to close my eyes and be surprised."

She settled into the seat, leaned her head back and closed her eyes.

What a wonderful day. Making love had been a beautiful beginning, and now, as the late-afternoon sun moved west, she could look back on the rest of it as near perfect.

Over brunch they'd finally cleared the air. Janelle admitted the truth of Tom's charge that she was afraid. Then added, "Somehow, admitting it out loud took care of it. I realized that it's better to love and maybe face loss than to live a sterile, safe existence."

It was more difficult for him to come to terms with his selfishness. It had been a form of self-protection for so long. "But I have no doubts that you'll keep me on an even keel. That common sense is one of the things that first attracted me." He smiled at her over the rim of his coffee cup. "That and your polished toenails."

The look had made those same toes curl.

Tom continued. "I thought long and hard about those 'unrealistic sacrifices' you accused me of."

She cringed a little as she remembered her harsh words. But Tom shrugged his shoulders. "You were right. After that, I put some real thought into what would work for me and for you. That's when I came up with the contract changes. The timing was right, and Harris was willing to pitch it for me and it worked.

"The way I figure it, we've got one more hurdle to cross." He put down his cup and took Janelle's hand. "God knows, I want to do this right." He closed his eyes for a moment and then nodded. "I once suggested that we live together. I want you to know now that I think that that was a monumentally stupid idea. I don't want to take the chance that one day you'll get so mad at my high-handedness that you'll just walk out. I thought maybe if we were married, you'd be willing to stick it out for the long haul."

Janelle smiled. He was trying so hard not to sound pushy but still trying to get her into a spot where she couldn't refuse. Well, she decided, he'd succeeded.

"Yes."

He was staring at their clasped hands and seemed not to hear her. "I don't want to rush you. But I thought you should know where I stand. Sometimes I know I move too fast for you—"

"Tom—" Janelle reached over and patted their clasped hands "—I said yes."

He stopped speaking immediately and then looked disconcerted. "But I don't have the ring yet."

"Well, if you want me to take the yes back, I can, but—"

"No way! We'll put ring shopping on the list, right after house hunting."

Tom swung around the corner with a squeal of brakes, snapping Janelle out of her reverie. "It's just two more blocks. What do you think?"

Now it was her turn to compromise. She breathed a prayer and opened her eyes. It was an established neighborhood with huge trees, their red and yellow leaves at the height of their fall color. It was picture perfect. It even reminded her a little of Jackson. The houses were newer and the yards smaller, but they reflected the same pride of ownership she found at home.

They rolled to a stop in front of a modest two-story house with a discreet For Sale sign on the corner of the property. Its siding was painted a light green with bright white trim. There was a jalousie-windowed porch on one side and a driveway leading to a garage that was a separate building but connected to the house by an enclosed breezeway.

Tom turned to Janelle expectantly. "What do you think?"

She turned to him, smiling. "I think it looks great. Is the inside as nice?"

It was. A conventional four bedrooms and three baths, the house was made special by a fabulous attic study, perfect for rainy days and snowy nights.

When Janelle saw the back veranda that ran the length of the house, she was sold. She turned to Tom. "This porch was made for root-beer floats."

He walked the length of the porch. "It really needs a couple of rocking chairs."

She walked into his arms and he held her close. "I'll tell you what, Tom. We can put those rocking chairs on the shopping list, right after rings."

"Nell, I know how much the house in Jackson means to you. I'd kind of like to keep it, wouldn't you? This yard really is too shady for a good vegetable garden and—"

She hushed him with a kiss. "Shh, you make it sound like living here with you would be some kind of sacrifice. If you want, we can stay in the other house. I could learn to love it, if you were there."

"That house means nothing to me. Here..." He paused, looking around the empty porch, and Janelle followed his eyes, picturing summer evenings with Dan and Tippy, growing up and growing old. "I think we could build a good life here—a life that lets our true colors show, and lets them grow and change together."

They walked back through the house more slowly this time, Tom running out of his real estate patter and beginning to talk more personally of their shared future and his hopes for it.

"You can help me keep my feet on the ground, and I'll inch you back into the big wide world. I know for sure you'll let me know when I push too hard."

Janelle nodded and smiled through a sheen of tears that did nothing to mask her happiness. Tom laughed at her sentimentality, pulling her close, kissing her eyelids and the trail of tears, resting his lips on her mouth.

He pushed her toward the door. "Come on, we're on a roll." He locked the door, grabbed her hand and pulled her

down the walk. "Let's not stop now. We've got a house.
What's next? The ring or the rocking chairs?"

*   *   *   *   *

Silhouette Desire

Don't miss the enchanting
TALES OF THE RISING MOON
A Desire trilogy by Joyce Thies

MOON OF THE RAVEN—June (#432)
Conlan Fox was part American Indian and as tough as the Montana land he rode, but it took fragile yet strong-willed Kerry Armstrong to make his dreams come true.

REACH FOR THE MOON—August (#444)
It would take a heart of stone for Steven Armstrong to evict the woman and children living on his land. But when Steven saw Samantha, eviction was the last thing on his mind!

GYPSY MOON—October (#456)
Robert Armstrong met Serena when he returned to his ancestral estate in Connecticut. Their fiery temperaments clashed from the start, but despite himself, Rob was falling under the Gypsy's spell.

 # Silhouette Desire

COMING
NEXT MONTH

#451 DESTINY'S CHILD—Ann Major
Book Two of *Children of Destiny*. Ten years ago Jeb Jackson had
become Megan MacKay's most hated enemy—but he was still the
man she'd never stopped loving.

#452 A MATCH MADE IN HEAVEN—Katherine Granger
Film reviewers Colin Cassidy and Gina Longford were at odds
from the moment they met. The sparks between them were
dynamite on television and explosive off!

#453 HIDE AND SEEK—Lass Small
When Tate Lambert had uncharacteristically thrown herself at
Bill Sawyer, he hadn't been interested. Two months later he had a
change of heart, but apparently so had she....

#454 SMOOTH OPERATOR—Helen R. Myers
Camilla Ryland checked into Max Lansing's tropical island resort
to get away from it all. But Max was a smooth operator, and he
wasn't about to let the beautiful actress "get away" from him.

#455 THE PRINCESS AND THE PEA—Kathleen Korbel
Princess Cassandra led a fairy-tale existence before she met the
handsome undercover agent Paul Phillips. He'd rescued her from
danger, and now they were fleeing for their lives.

#456 GYPSY MOON—Joyce Thies
The third of three *Tales of the Rising Moon*. Veterinarian Robert
Armstrong didn't intend to get involved with a wild gypsy
woman. But then he met Serena Danvers and fell under her spell.

AVAILABLE NOW:

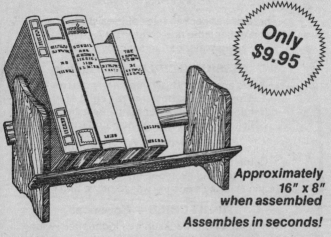

Silhouette Desire®

CHILDREN OF DESTINY

A trilogy by Ann Major

Three power-packed tales of irresistible passion and undeniable fate created by Ann Major to wrap your heart in a legacy of love.

PASSION'S CHILD — September

Years ago, Nick Browning nearly destroyed Amy's life, but now that the child of his passion—the child of her heart—was in danger, Nick was the only one she could trust....

DESTINY'S CHILD — October

Cattle baron Jeb Jackson thought he owned everything and everyone on his ranch, but fiery Megan MacKay's destiny was to prove him wrong!

NIGHT CHILD — November

When little Julia Jackson was kidnapped, young Kirk MacKay blamed himself. Twenty years later, he found her... and discovered that love could shine through even the darkest of nights.

Don't miss PASSION'S CHILD, DESTINY'S CHILD and NIGHT CHILD, three thrilling Silhouette Desires designed to heat up chilly autumn nights!

SD-445